On the face of it, after her tycoon husband's death Olivia had the world as her oyster: a rich and powerful widow, she could do anything she wanted. Anything—except have the love of the only man in the world she could ever love.

SMOKESCREEN

BY

ANNE MATHER

MILLS & BOON LIMITED
15–16 BROOK'S MEWS
LONDON W1A 1DR

First published 1982
Australian copyright 1982
Philippine copyright 1982
This edition 1982

© Anne Mather 1982

ISBN 0 263 73796 9

Set in Monophoto Times 10 on 11 pt.
01–0482

Made and printed in Great Britain by Richard Clay (The Chaucer Press) Ltd, Bungay, Suffolk

CHAPTER ONE

'THE Lord giveth, and the Lord taketh away ... ashes to ashes, dust to dust ...'

The words of the funeral service drifted over Olivia's head. She was hardly aware of them. She was hardly aware of the sunny February day, an inappropriate contrast to the sombreness of the occasion, or of the covertly interested glances she attracted, as the young, bereaved widow. She appeared unconcerned that her sallow skin and ebony black hair were a startling contrast in this essentially English setting, or that the sable coat she wore with such indifference accentuated her almost alien appearance. She seemed remote from what was happening around her, careless that her manner might be misconstrued; the whispered speculations of her fellow mourners reaching her ears with no more consequence than the sound of the leaves shifting about her feet.

There were a great number of mourners gathered about the graveside, associates and business colleagues of Henry Gantry, his fellow directors in the huge chemical corporation he had founded, employees; anyone who thought that by being there they might prove themselves in some way. Henry Gantry had been a powerful man, in death he still commanded great respect, and although not one of them would admit to being afraid of him, they all had been, at one time or another.

Olivia was the exception. She had not been afraid of him. She had hated him before she even knew him, and latterly she had come to despise him, and herself. But fear, that was for people whose lives Henry Gantry had been able to control, and there had been many, she had to admit. Yet, strangely enough, living in his house, she had come close to respecting him, even if she could never forgive him for what he had done. She had even discovered in herself a mild contempt for people whose weaknesses Henry had exploited. It was a feeling she had fought to overcome, and now it was all over. Or perhaps it was only beginning . . .

The funeral service had ended. The heavy, lead-lined coffin had been lowered into the ground, and Francis Kennedy, who had been Henry Gantry's personal assistant, touched her sleeve.

'Let me drive you back to the house, Mrs Gantry,' he offered, with the bland personable charm that seemed to have ensured his success with her sex. 'You must be cold and tired. What you need is a stiff brandy—to take the strain.'

Olivia turned her long green eyes in his direction, their cool transparency startling in those dark features. 'Thank you,' she said, civilly enough, although experience had taught her to distrust too much subservience. 'I think I can stand it, Francis. I shall ride back with Forsyth, as usual. As you can see, he's waiting for me. But it was a nice gesture.'

Francis Kennedy inclined his head. 'It was my pleasure, Mrs Gantry. I'll see you later, at the house.'

Olivia acknowledged his submission and then, with a faint smile for the priest who had conducted the ceremony, she turned in the direction of the cars. Poor Father Donovan, she thought cynically, as the heels of her long boots sank into the soggy turf that flanked the graves. Like everyone else, he had succumbed to the corrosive power of wealth and possession, and although Henry Gantry had never stepped inside a church in his life, his funeral Mass had been just as magnificent as that conveyed to the most ardent believer. But perhaps that was only right, she reflected, forcing her callousness aside. What was it she had read: that God rejoiced more over the repentance of one non-believer than over so many who had had faith? She shook her head. It was something like that. The trouble was, Henry Gantry had repented nothing. He had lived his life the way he chose to live it, and at the end he had had only gratification for his own shrewd reasoning.

The sun was hidden by a cloud suddenly, and the bright afternoon with its promise of spring became at once dull and overcast. Although it was barely three o'clock, it would be dark soon, and Olivia quickened her step to where the chauffeur, Forsyth, was standing beside the Rolls.

A flutter of condolences surrounded her as Forsyth opened the door of the Rolls for Olivia to ascend. Malcolm Birk, Henry's managing director, and his wife, pressed forward to offer their regrets, Barry Freeman, the company secretary, Sean Barrett, another director; Mortimer Lloyd, Lane Grimond, Paul Sloane, James Farrell; Olivia acknowledged all their commiserations with unsmiling politeness, aware as she did so that each one of them was concerned for his own ends and no one else. Henry had been right about one thing, she thought, sinking back against the soft leather upholstery; they were like a pack of wolves, intent on the kill. And if her position had not been so secure, she would have been the first casualty.

Expelling her breath on a sigh, she became aware of Forsyth's eyes watching her through the rear-view mirror. But his eyes showed concern, not avarice, and she allowed a slight smile to touch her lips in answer to his unspoken question.

'I'll be all right,' she said, drawing off the black suede gloves which had hidden her narrow fingers. Examining the square-cut sapphire that nudged the broad gold wedding band on her left hand, she shook her head half disbelievingly. 'I'll be all right, Forsyth,' she said again. 'You'll see.'

There were reporters at the gates of the cemetery, a gaggle of them, with notebooks and cameras, leaning dangerously close to the car as it passed to take yet another picture of the grieving widow. For it was quite a news story: a young woman, of only twenty-two years of age, whose marriage to a man more than forty years her senior had made her a celebrity; a bride of only six months, widowed by her elderly bridegroom, and suddenly one of the wealthiest women in the world.

Olivia could not hide from the flashing light bulbs, so she did not try. She sat there, cool and remote, her intense composure yet another source of speculation for the gossip-hungry readers of the gutter press. She knew everyone thought she had married Henry for his money, and she supposed she had, in a way. But not in the way they meant; not even in the way his business associates believed; and certainly not for the reasons Henry himself had put forward.

It was only a fifteen-minute drive from St Saviour's cemetery to the house she had shared with Henry for the past six months. They had not had a honeymoon; it would have been an unbearable irony. And in any case, Henry had already been a sick man. He had known the few months he had left to him, and while Olivia might despise his memory, she could not help but admire the strength of will which had kept this knowledge in the back of his mind. Only his closest associates, like Francis Kennedy, had been aware that ill health had impaired his ability to function as he would have liked. But who would have believed it, after all? He had been a fighter to the last. And only the gauntness of his features in these last few weeks had betrayed the hours of pain he had suffered in silence. He had always looked so strong;

a fine figure of a man, with his broad shoulders and tall physique. Indeed, when the pictures of their wedding appeared in the papers, not everyone had envied him his good fortune. Some had envied Olivia too, and not just because Henry Gantry was reputed to be the fifteenth most wealthy man in the world.

The Rolls slowed as they turned into Virginia Drive, and the tall steel gates of the house confronted them. Virginia Drive wasn't really a road at all, it was a cul-de-sac, with only the high walls of Henry Gantry's property on either side. The gates, which were set squarely at the end, guarded the entrance to the private estate, and were patrolled day and night by armed guards with dogs. As the Rolls approached, it was identified, and the heavy steel gates swung back with mechanised smoothness. Olivia received a polite salute from the guard on duty as she passed, and although in the beginning she had been embarrassed by this mark of respect, now she raised her hand automatically, without even giving it much thought.

A gravelled sweep curved between tall hydrangeas and rhododendron bushes, before emerging into the wide forecourt before the house. The house itself was casually elegant, a neo-Georgian edifice, with a pillared portico and panelled doors below a fluted fanlight. A series of box hedges gave definition to the terrace, and beyond them a manicured expanse of lawn, inset with a lily pool and flower beds, provided a formal display. Everywhere was immaculate, as immaculate as an army of gardeners could make it, and because Henry Gantry had believed in paying for service, he had never suffered from any shortage of staff.

'Will you be wanting the car again today, Mrs Gantry?'

Forsyth's polite enquiry drew Olivia's attention, and she looked at him almost absently. She had been absorbed with her thoughts, absorbed with the enormity of the task that confronted her, and Forsyth's simple question required some concentration.

'No,' she said at last. 'No, I don't think so, thank you, Forsyth. You can take the rest of the day off.'

'Why, thank you, Mrs Gantry.' Forsyth was pleasantly surprised. He walked round the car and opened the door for her as she moved to alight. 'Take it easy, hmm?' he added, as she accepted his hand, and the sympathy he had shown her in the car was renewed in that warm grasp.

'Thank you.' Only briefly, her rare smile showed, and then she released herself and walked towards the house as other cars pulled up behind them.

The hall of the house was high-ceilinged and wide, carpeted in blue and gold, and supporting a huge chandelier. There were other lights, set around the walls, whose discreet positioning highlighted some of the many original paintings Henry Gantry had collected during his business career; and as they were presently lit to allay the gloom of the lowering skies, the hall had a warmth and an intimacy it was sometimes lacking.

The house itself was built on two levels. Where Olivia stood to allow the butler, Hamish Murdoch, to help her to remove her coat was the upper level, and to either side of her, the drawing rooms and the library opened on to this level. The stairs, that gave access to the first floor, also rose along one panelled wall, and the gallery above provided further space for Henry's collection.

Ahead of her, Olivia could see the sweeping arch that framed the shallow steps that led down to the dining room and sun lounge, and her late husband's study. This part of the house faced south, and a series of glass doors in each of the rooms gave access to a pool patio, which Henry had used frequently when the weather was good enough. Below the patio, the ground fell away gradually to the river, the Thames at this point being deep enough and wide enough to create a natural barrier to intruders.

A cold buffet had been laid in one of the drawing rooms, at Olivia's suggestion. She had not wanted a formal gathering in the dining room, and besides, this way no one would notice how little she ate. Francis Kennedy, typically, was the first to arrive, and he surreptitiously took over, organising drinks for those who wanted them, and generally taking the pressure off Olivia. She knew she would feel grateful to him, for easing her position, if only she could stop thinking of the motives behind his conciliatory smile.

Henry's solicitor was there; Adam Cosgrove had known Henry all his working life, and Olivia supposed it wasn't unreasonable that he should feel some remorse. Nevertheless, she thought he looked at her with more than a degree of calculation, and she wondered if he was speculating how best to present his suit. It was a little distracting to consider how many people had depended on Henry for their livelihood, and who now depended on her! How would they feel when they learned what she intended to do? She was realistic enough to know that they would not admire her for it.

'Olivia!'

A woman's faintly sardonic voice spoke behind her, and she turned to confront Drusilla Stone. The other woman looked cool and elegant, in a dark fur coat over plain grey flannel, her immaculately tinted hair as fair as Olivia's was dark. She certainly didn't look her age, Olivia reflected bitterly, and no doubt of all Henry's retainers, Drusilla would benefit most; but perhaps that was how it should be; she had been his mistress for years, and had remained so up until his marriage.

'Hello, Drusilla,' Olivia responded now, without expression. 'So good of you to come. I knew you would.'

Drusilla's lips twisted. 'It was the least I could do, don't you think? For Henry's memory? Of all the hangers-on here, including yourself, I have the most right to expect an acknowledgement.'

Olivia did not take offence. She knew Drusilla had never forgiven Henry for marrying someone else, particularly someone so much younger than herself.

'I don't suppose you'll be disappointed, Drusilla,' she remarked now, offering her a canapé from the tray held by a passing waitress. And when the older woman refused: 'Surely we can overlook our differences now. We have so much in common.

'I have nothing in common with a money-grubbing little gold-digger like you!' Drusilla hissed venomously. 'And if Henry hadn't been so all-fired keen to deprive that selfish son of his from getting his hands on his money, he'd never have been taken in by an over-sexed little——'

'That's enough, don't you think?' Francis Kennedy's smooth interruption successfully circumvented Drusilla's attack. 'Dear Drusilla! You never could distinguish between good taste and bad, could you? And don't you think H.R. knew that? Or else you'd be standing where Olivia's standing now.'

Drusilla's carefully painted face contorted. 'Keep out of this, Kennedy! Don't think I can't see your game! With Henry dead, you've got to revise your strategy, haven't you? And paying court to his rich widow must have its attractions.'

Kennedy's expression hardly changed, but his eyes narrowed angrily and Olivia sighed as she put a hand on his arm. 'Please, Francis,' she said, 'it's kind of you to defend me, but honestly, I can look after myself.'

'Yes, she can look after herself, *Francis*!' Drusilla mocked maliciously. 'You'd better believe it. She's Mrs Gantry, and you and I aren't even poor relations!'

'Shut up, Drusilla——'

'Oh, please! Can't we leave it?' Olivia's fingers tightened round the stem on her glass. 'This is my husband's funeral, Francis. I'd appreciate it if you'd remember that. Perhaps you'd make sure everyone has what they need. You know them all so much better than I do.

'Certainly, Mrs Gantry.'

Francis resumed his role smoothly, and ignoring Drusilla's malevolent gaze, he quickly circulated among the guests. Olivia, for her part, was relieved when several other members of the gathering joined them, and Drusilla eventually drifted away, no doubt to brood over past injustices.

Olivia managed to handle the conversation adroitly. Even in so short a time she had learned to dissemble, and it was easier to accept these people at their face value than try to evaluate their individual intentions. She knew they were wary of her. She knew they were suspicious of her plans now that Henry was dead. It could not be easy, having a stranger thrust so unexpectedly into their midst, a stranger moreover who had been given the power to direct the future course of their lives.

'Well, Olivia——' It was Adam Cosgrove at her side, his lined face grave and thoughtful. 'I suggest we get the formalities over with, don't you? I realise you may not be feeling up to it right now, but these matters have to be attended to, I'm afraid. If you'd like to join me in the library, I think we can suitably dispose of H.R.'s last wishes.'

Olivia's features stiffened. 'You've read the will?'

'As I helped to draw it up, of course.'

'Of course.' Olivia felt foolish. 'When—when was this?'

'A few days after your marriage.' Adam was prosaic. 'But you knew. Surely H.R. told you what he planned to do?'

'Oh, yes.' Olivia's tongue appeared to moisten her lips. 'Yes, he told me. I only wondered——'

'——whether he'd kept his word?' suggested Adam sagely. 'Well, that rather depends on what limitations you expected, I suppose. You're a very rich young woman, but I'm sure you know that. As for the rest——'

'The rest? You mean Henry's estate?'

'I mean his estate, of course. His shares in the corporation; his interests in banking and mining; his involvement in the development of North Sea oil; his houses, here, and in New York and the South of France; his collection; his racehorses——'

'Oh, don't go on.' Olivia pressed the palm of one hand to her cheek, the delicate shade of her nail varnish so much warmer then the pallor of her skin. She felt chilled, inside and out, and even swallowing the last of her brandy could not remove the sense of apprehension that was gripping her now the moment had come.

'Very well.' Adam bowed his head in silent acceptance of her plea. 'I suggest we continue this conversation in more private circumstances. Will you lead the way? I want to speak to Kennedy.'

The library was empty, but Mrs Winters had had a fire laid in the wide hearth and its flames were welcoming. The library was the only room in the house that possessed a chimney, and Olivia had spent many hours here, examining the books that lined two walls. The curtains had been drawn against the darkness that was now complete, and their plummy velvet folds provided a fitting backcloth to the heavy desk that stood squarely in front of them.

Olivia paced about the room anxiously as she waited, her fingers playing with the double rope of pearls that circled her slender throat. They were real pearls, just as the diamonds in her ears were real diamonds, and the simple jersey dress she wore had cost a fortune in a Paris fashion house. Henry Gantry was nothing if not thorough, and he had made Olivia his wife in every possible way. She had to look like his wife, as well as act like it, and money was no object to a man of his means.

It seemed hours before Adam joined her, but a glance at the exquisitely designed watch on her wrist confirmed that it was scarcely five minutes. The watch was accurate to two seconds in five years, or some such ridiculous claim, but in this instance it was enough to know that it was her tenseness that had made time drag.

She had expected he would have brought Francis with him, and perhaps Drusilla, too, but he had not. Adam was alone as he closed the door behind him, and its heavy soundproofed panels ensured their conversation the utmost privacy.

'Won't you sit down?' Adam placed his briefcase on the desk, and surveyed her slim figure with mild impatience. 'My dear, there's absolutely no need to look so apprehensive.' His lips curled a little wryly. 'You are H.R.'s heir, in spite of my pleas on Alex's behalf. Relax. There's not a court in England that could overthrow it.'

Olivia sank down into a dark green leather armchair. It was strange, hearing Alex Gantry's name spoken for the first time in this house. Henry had never used it. If he had ever mentioned his offspring, it was always as 'that ungrateful whelp' or 'Elise's brat', and just occasionally as 'that bastard son of mind'. Olivia had never troubled to work out what it was that Alex had done to deserve his father's undying hatred. But if Henry had disowned him, it must have been something pretty bad. It was no concern of hers, she thought, moving her shoulders in a dismissing gesture. She had not been responsible for Henry's decision to cut his son out of his will. She had been merely the unwilling instrument of that decision, and she should not feel remorse now when her revenge was within her grasp. Henry Gantry had been an unscrupulous man, it was right and fitting that he, in his turn, should have been taken in by an unscrupulous woman; though whether she was as strong in her convictions as he had been, remained to be seen.

'You seem—distracted, Olivia.' Adam was speaking again, and she looked up at him almost blankly, aware that for several minutes she had been absorbed with her thoughts. 'Is something wrong?' he persisted. 'You're not—afraid of the responsibilities that are now yours? You needn't be, you know. You have some of the best business brains in the world to help you.'

Olivia shook her head. If he only knew, she thought with irony. 'I was thinking,' she excused herself quickly. 'I'm sorry, Mr Cosgrove. What were you saying?'

Adam hesitated. 'You haven't—that is—there's been no word from Alex, I suppose?'

'Alex?' Olivia blinked. 'No. Should there have been?'

'Well—no,' Adam shrugged. 'Was he informed?'

'As I have no idea where he is, that would have been difficult,' Olivia replied tautly. 'Henry said something about his living in Africa, but Africa's a big place, and he never heard from him.'

'No.' Adam nodded. 'No, of course not.' He flicked open the lid of his briefcase. 'Shall we begin?'

Olivia scarcely listened to the preamble. It wasn't long. Henry had no close relatives, other than herself and Alex, of course, and his bequests to the members of his staff were characteristically few. Five hundred pounds here, a thousand pounds there; Francis Kennedy received a bonus in the form of a five-thousand-pound block of shares in Gantry Chemicals; but otherwise the vast sum of his estate remained intact, to be administered by his wife, Olivia, *providing certain conditions were adhered to.*

Olivia straightened her spine. 'What conditions?' she asked Adam, her green eyes alight with suspicion, and the elderly lawyer exhaled a sigh before explaining the situation.

'It's quite simple,' he said. 'I don't think you'll find them onerous. H.R. simply wanted to ensure that his business empire survived his death.'

Olivia sprang to her feet. 'You said the estate was mine!'

'I said you were his heir,' said Adam mildly, his eyes showing faint bewilderment. 'My dear, surely you consider an income of some quarter of a million pounds a year an adequate commission for sustaining Henry's controlling interest in the Gantry corporation?'

'What are you saying?' Olivia gazed at him. 'That I can't dispose of it?'

Adam looked confused. 'Why should you wish to do that? Olivia, you'll have everything anyone could ever want—money, power, position——'

'But not complete power,' she exclaimed harshly 'You're saying that the estate is entailed.'

Adam regarded her with evident perplexity. 'My dear, you'd be a fool to sell, even if you were able to do so. In this time of recession, the corporation has continued to make a comfortable profit for its shareholders, and now that the economic crisis seems to be bottoming out——'

'I know all that.' Olivia turned away, her hands pressed to her cheeks, a sick sense of defeat replacing the nervous anticipation inside her. God, she had been a fool! Her mother had been a fool! They should have known that Henry would find some way to perpetuate his memory. It had been naïve to imagine he would give her complete control. He had alleviated his conscience. He had left her well provided for. But the capital investment remained within his grasp, even after death.

'There is one more thing.' Adam spoke tentatively,

his tone indicating his continuing mystification at her attitude. 'It concerns the future, Olivia. If—if you should decide to get married again, your position as nominal head of the corporation will be withdrawn. You will receive a settlement of three hundred thousand pounds, but your controlling interest will, at that time, be taken into trust for H.R.'s grandchildren, should Alex ever produce any.'

Olivia steeled herself to look at him. 'And this house?'

'All H.R.'s houses are yours, so long as you wish to live in them,' replied Adam.

'But—if I marry?'

'Again the situation changes. The houses are part of the Gantry estate.'

Olivia nodded. She felt immensely weary suddenly. It seemed as if it had all been for nothing, she thought painfully. Her mother's schemes, her mother's desire for revenge—it had all been futile. Oh, she was wealthy now, more wealthy than she had any right to be, and that was part of her disillusionment. She had not wanted to be wealthy. She had not wanted Henry's money. And although at the time it had seemed a cruel irony, perhaps it was as well now that her mother would never learn how unnecessary her sacrifice had been. In her confused state, she might well have suspected Olivia of being a party to this all along.

It was so unfair! For a moment, a tearful sense of outrage gripped her. She had given up her career, her future, her life! Maybe another girl would have found it fair recompense. Olivia did not. She had been inveigled into a marriage that was abhorrent to her, persuaded it was the only way to restore her mother's health, only to find that Henry's desire to make amends had been as empty as his proposal. He had only wanted a scapegoat, she could see that now, someone to deprive his son of his inheritance.

Adam folded the will and laid the copy in his briefcase. Then he said stiffly: 'I suggest you sleep on it,
Olivia. Obviously, this is neither the time nor the place
to go into further detail. Perhaps you'd allow me to
make an appointment for you to come and see me in a
day or so. We can continue this discussion at that
time.'

'Wait——' Olivia put out her hand instinctively, forcing a note of apology into her tone. After all, this was
not Adam's fault, and it would not serve any purpose
she had to make an enemy of Henry's trusted business
advisor. 'I—I want to thank you,' she said, adopting a
rueful expression. 'I'm afraid you must think me very
ungrateful. It's just that—well, I suppose the fact of
Henry's death hasn't really sunk in yet.'

That was an outright lie, and she thought that perhaps
Adam identified it as such. But he was evidently
prepared to give her the benefit of the doubt, and he
took her hand automatically as he made his farewells.
His attitude gave Olivia pause, and almost incredulously
she realised that so far as Adam was concerned, she still
wielded a hefty weapon. Henry had given her the power
to administer his controlling interest; how she actually
used that power was her decision to make. She could be
the symbolic, but silent, partner they expected, or she
could exercise her rights to offer her opinion. How far
that opinion would be listened to remained to be seen,
but one thing seemed certain: no one, not Adam
Cosgrove, or Francis Kennedy, and most particularly
not Henry himself would expect her to involve herself in
the corporation's affairs.

Adam left, not altogether satisfied, she knew, with
her explanation, but prepared to put it down to the inconsistency of her being female. His departure seemed
to signal to the others that it was time they, too, made

their farewells, and in ones and twos they took to their cars, their expressions of sympathy ringing in Olivia's ears long after the steel gates had sealed behind them.

Francis had left, too, after offering to remain behind and being refused. He had suggested she might need company over dinner, but as Olivia had little taste for food right now, she had declined his proposal.

'It's very kind of you, Francis,' she said, 'but I'd prefer to be alone. I—have a lot to think about. We'll talk again in the morning. Join me for breakfast. I—I have something I want to talk to you about.'

He had been curious, she had known that, and vaguely wary of any proposition she might devolve. But like Adam before him, he was sufficiently in awe of her position not to argue, and Olivia had known an unexpected surge of excitement as she flexed the reins of power for the first time.

It was only as she was leaving that Olivia remembered Drusilla. The other woman had not been mentioned among the few bequests Henry had made, and Olivia felt a wave of compassion sweep over her for the bitterness Drusilla must be feeling. It was typical of Henry Gantry, of course. He never forgot an insult, and Drusilla's behaviour at the time of his marriage had created an unpleasant scene.

'I'm sorry,' Olivia said quietly, as Mrs Stone passed her on her way out to her car. She made no further explanations. None was necessary. But Drusilla was not prepared to accept her dismissal gracefully.

'You will be,' she declared spitefully, her eyes glittering. 'One day you're going to regret you ever laid eyes on Henry Gantry, and you can be sure I'll be around to see it!'

Olivia found she was trembling when the door finally closed behind the last of her guests, and the housekeeper, Mrs Winters, exchanged a knowing look with

Hamish Murdoch. Surprisingly enough, the members of the household staff had all grown to like and respect the young Mrs Gantry, and her quiet manner and unassuming ways had won her many friends among their ranks.

'It's been too much for you, Mrs Gantry,' the housekeeper exclaimed, but Olivia resisted her efforts to urge her back into the library. 'I said it would be, and I've been proved right. You look as if every drop of blood has drained out of you!'

Olivia managed a faint smile for both of them. 'I'm all right, really,' she assured them. 'Just—tired, I think.' She paused. 'I think I'll take a bath before dinner. Do you think I could eat from a tray this evening? I really don't feel like facing the dining room alone.'

'Why don't you get straight into bed, and I'll get Mary to bring it up for you?' Murdoch suggested, but Olivia shook her head.

'I'll come down,' she said firmly. 'I don't feel like going to bed right now. I'll probably watch television for a while. After you've arranged about the meal, you can all take the rest of the night off.'

It was a relief to reach the sanctuary of her room. It was such a beautiful apartment, and at least one area of the house which held no associations of Henry. Oh, he had probably hired the interior decorators who had designed it for her, she reflected, sinking down on to the side of the huge square bed; but he had never entered the room during her habitation, and she had made it peculiarly her own by the addition of her personal possessions.

Her brushes, with their gilt handles, did look a little out of place on the crystal tray on her dressing table, but she didn't care. She wasn't ashamed of her background, and she had refused to pretend she was used to such luxury as she now possessed. Perhaps this was one of the reasons why the servants had taken such a liking to her; because she had never hidden the fact that she had been brought up in surroundings similar to theirs.

Nevertheless, she had become fond of the exquisitely appointed rooms allocated to her. She would not have been human if she had not appreciated a superbly-sprung mattress and real silk sheets, that stroked her skin with sensuous enjoyment; she would not have been honest if she had denied the pleasures of waking up in the morning to the artistic beauty of linen-covered walls, in delicious shades of rose and turquoise, and a soft, shaggy carpet to tease her toes; and she would not have been feminine if she had not felt a thrill every time she slid back the doors of the air-conditioned units in her dressing room, to disclose the rows and rows of suits and dresses, pants and skirts and sweaters and jeans, enough to last a lifetime, were fashion never to change.

Now, Olivia bent and unzipped her boots, kicking them off carelessly as she stood to unfasten the tiny pearl buttons of her dress. When she pushed it off her shoulders, it fell too, in a pool of silk jersey about her feet, and picking it up she tossed it on to the bed. Her reflection, in the stark simplicity of her black slip, was thrown back at her from half a dozen mirrors set about the room, but she paid little attention to her appearance. She saw little to admire in her magnolia-pale skin and night-dark hair. Her mother's Italian ancestry was never more pronounced than when she was tired, and she turned aside impatiently and strode into the bathroom.

She ran her own bath, liberally sprinkling the contents of a cut-glass flagon of perfumed essence into the water. The step-in tub was deep and wide, and she filled it almost to the brim before stepping into its scented softness, feeling the chill that had enveloped her dispersing in its warmth. She must not allow herself to become depressed, she thought determinedly. She was still the nominal head of the Gantry corporation. And tomorrow she would find out from Francis exactly what that meant.

She was seated on the padded stool in front of her dressing table brushing her hair when there was a knock at her door, and a young woman's voice called: 'It's me, Mrs Gantry. Can I come in?'

'Of course, Mary.' Olivia forced herself to welcome the young woman who entered, even though she would have preferred to be alone.

'You should have asked me to run your bath for you, Mrs Gantry,' Mary Parrish exclaimed reprovingly, picking up Olivia's discarded dress and slipping it on to its hanger. 'How are you feeling now? Mrs Winters seemed to think you had overdone it. Why don't you get into bed, and let me fetch you some supper?'

'Thank you, Mary, but I prefer to eat downstairs,' declared Olivia resignedly, wishing the girl didn't take her duties so seriously. Henry had employed her, soon after their marriage, to act as lady's maid, and Olivia had often wished he had consulted her first. However, she meant well, and Olivia tempered her remark with a small smile so that she should not hurt Mary's feelings.

'Then what are you going to wear, Mrs Gantry?' the girl persisted, carrying the silk jersey into the dressing room and replacing it in the closet. 'I suggest this trouser suit,' she displayed an outfit consisting of narrow fitting pants and knee-length jacket, teamed with a silk shirt, 'or this,' which was a soft cashmere caftan, with knee-length slits at either side.

Olivia sighed. She had considered going downstairs in a dressing gown and pyjamas, but she realised there was always the possibility that someone else might call to offer their condolences. She could always plead a headache, of course, and avoid visitors, but with Mary pulling out various combinations of garments, it was easier to choose than explain her preference.

'The caftan, I think,' she said, indicating the exquisite handwork of the knitted cashmere. Its muted shades of blue and mauve were suitably restrained, and she cared little that it was one of the most flattering items in her wardrobe.

'I wish I had a figure like yours, Mrs Gantry,' Mary remarked later, when the folds of the caftan clung lovingly to Olivia's shapely form. Indeed, its plain lines accentuated the rounded swell of her bosom, and displayed the slimness of her hips and the slender length of her legs.

Olivia shook her head, unconvinced in spite of Mary's sincerity. 'Clothes maketh man—or woman,' she misquoted, half cynically. 'Leave my hair loose, Mary. I shan't be seeing anyone tonight.'

Leaving the maid to tidy the room, Olivia descended the stairs with slow deliberation. It was strange to think this house was hers, so long as she chose to live in it, unmarried, of course; the rooms were hers to decorate as she wished; the servants were hers to command. It was a tempting proposition, as Henry had known it would be. He had left her enough money, whatever her inclination, to live in luxury for the rest of her life; firmly believing, as he had always believed, that personal gratification was all that mattered.

But it wasn't. Not for her. She had not married Henry Gantry to embrace his philosophy. Her motives might have been thwarted at every turn, but she was still determined not to give in. Her mother was dead. She could no longer help her. But she could help the one person Henry had least desired to benefit from his fortune: his son!

Her feet sank into the rich pile of the hall carpet as she walked towards the library. Mrs Winters would know where to find her; the library had become her retreat from Henry's world. Opening the door, she found the lamps still burning and the fire replenished. Its visible warmth was comforting, and she closed the door wearily, leaning back against it, and closing her eyes.

When she opened them again, the first thing she saw was a pair of booted feet set apart on the hearthrug; and as her eyes moved unsteadily upward, they quickly covered long denim-clad legs and thighs, a loose fitting jersey over an open-necked denim shirt, and a lean tanned face below a straight slick of ash-streaked hair. The man was leanly built, but his chest was broad, and the vee of his shirt revealed a gold medallion glinting among the fine whorls of body hair. His arms were strong and his legs looked powerful, and Olivia could not help but notice the bulging muscles of his thighs. But she did not know him. She had never seen him before in her life. And her initial reaction was that he must be an intruder, who had known he would find her alone.

However, before her undisciplined fears could take verbal form, he spoke, and when he did so, she suddenly realised his identity.

'Hello, Olivia,' he greeted her sardonically. 'How delightful to meet you at last. I'll say one thing for old Henry, he certainly had good taste!'

CHAPTER TWO

'*Alex!*'

The man inclined his head. 'How did you guess?'

Olivia straightened away from the door. 'How—how did you get in? Did Mrs Winters——'

'I let myself in,' he responded laconically, putting his hand into his pocket and pulling out a key, allowing it to hang from its silver chain like some kind of hypnotic device. 'Do I need an invitation? To Henry Gantry's house?'

Olivia struggled for composure. 'No. No, of course not.'

'Of course not,' he mocked, putting the key back into his pocket and indicating the leather armchairs set at either side of the fire. 'Won't you sit down—*Mother*? You look as if you need some support.'

Olivia looked at him uneasily, moistening her lips with a nervous tongue. This was a contingency she had not prepared herself for, and in spite of her half-formed intentions to try and find Henry's son, she was shaken to the core of her being by his unheralded appearance.

'When did you arrive?' she ventured. 'When did you get here? Do—do you know——'

'—that Henry's dead?' he finished flatly. 'Yes, I know. Cosgrove informed me.'

'Adam Cosgrove?' Olivia gazed at him, then shook her head. Of course. Adam had asked her if she had heard from Alex. He had obviously been aware of his whereabouts and informed him accordingly.

She stepped across the Persian carpet now, and determinedly held out her hand. Whatever her impressions, she had to conduct this first interview calmly, even if his expression did not encourage a closer liaison.

'Hello, Alex,' she said now, and after a moment's consideration he shook her hand. 'I'm sorry you had to learn about your father's death so abruptly. He'd been ill for some time, and it was not unexpected.'

'So I believe.'

Alex held on to her hand rather longer than was necessary, and Olivia had to pull it away before crossing to the desk and seating herself beside it. She felt more sure of herself sitting down, less vulnerable somehow; and she needed that space between them, to recover her sensibilities.

'You've been living in Africa, I believe,' she remarked, trying to keep her tone light. 'As we didn't know your address, we—I—had no way of contacting you.'

'Cosgrove knew where I was,' he pointed out dryly.

'Yes, obviously. But unfortunately he didn't tell me.'

Alex shrugged, pulling out a crumpled pack of cheroots. 'Do you mind?' he asked, and after gaining her permission, he added: 'I've been living in Tsaba for the past eight years. Do you know it? My—partner and I set up a mining company. Some of these central African republics are rich in mineral wealth.'

Olivia nodded. She was quite prepared to believe he had lived in rougher circumstances than these. There was a roughness about him, a hard virility, that seemed out of place in this elegant room. He looked as if he would feel more at home in the raw civilisation of a mining community, although she had to admit he did not seem at all concerned that his appearance did not match his surroundings.

'Can I get you a drink?' he offered, and she noticed the empty glass standing on the curve of the fender. He must have been sitting in one of the armchairs by the fire when she entered the room, she thought incredulously, but she had been so wrapped up in her thoughts, she had not noticed him.

'Thank you, no,' she said now, realising as she did so that it was she who should have made that remark. Summoning her most cordial tone, she said; 'Tell me, where are you staying? If I'd known you were coming——'

'—you'd have had the welcome mat out, I'm sure,' Alex cut in mockingly, his eyes, which were amazingly dark in his tanned face, narrowed and insolent. 'You surprise me, Olivia. I never expected such civility. I'd have thought you'd have kicked me out by now.'

Olivia's pale face gained colour. 'Then you're wrong, aren't you?'

'I don't know.' He studied her intently. 'I guess you knew how old Henry felt about his son.'

Olivia expelled her breath cautiously. 'Yes, I knew.'

He sneered. 'But you're prepared to be generous.'

'Henry's dead——'

'Too right.'

'—and I see no reason why we should not behave like civilised human beings——'

'The hell you don't!' Alex's lips curled.

'As—as I was saying,' Olivia continued determinedly, 'we can hardly be enemies when we don't even know one another.'

'Can't we?'

He was not making it easy for her, and Olivia wished she was more prepared for this interview. She should have had her speech written, her arguments marshalled; as it was, she was stumbling and faltering like a schoolgirl up before the head.

'I see no point in prolonging past grievances,' she declared steadily. 'Your father's dead. I don't know what happened between you two, but whatever it was, it had nothing to do with me.'

'Is that a fact?' Alex's lips were white now. 'So what's your game?'

'My game?' Olivia was speechless.

'Yes, Livvy, your game! God, my turning up here like this gave you one hell of a start, didn't it? My God! You must have thought you had it made. Henry's heiress, inheriting all this!' He waved a careless hand towards the ceiling. 'You're cool, I'll give you that. In your place, I'd have thrown you out and asked questions afterwards. But you—you're cleverer than that, aren't you? You must have been to hook old Henry in the first place. You realised straight off that my intervention might, just might, upset the applecart, so you've decided it might be safer to play both ends against the middle!'

'No!' Olivia was indignant, but Alex didn't believe her.

'No?' he mocked. 'You're not even the tiniest bit concerned that I might bring this house of cards down about your pretty ears!'

'No!'

'No what? No, you're not concerned, or no, you don't believe I can do it?' He took an indolent step towards her, and it was all Olivia could do to remain sitting in her seat under that insolent regard.

'I mean—no, you couldn't overset the will,' she said, through tight lips. 'It's tied up too securely for that. Didn't Adam tell you? He drew it up, on your father's instructions, of course.'

Alex's dark eyes narrowed speculatively. 'Livvy, you know as well as I do that in any civilised society, a man's heirs are his sons, not his wife.'

'Henry obviously did not consider he had a son——'

'A court of law might not agree with you.'

'I don't care what a court of law might think.' Olivia fought to defend herself. 'The will is watertight, Mr

Gantry. Henry was far too astute not to have considered every possibility.'

Alex snorted. 'What you mean is, you've got expensive tastes as well as greedy fingers!' he snapped. 'You're scared to death someone's going to come along and take a slice of it away from you!'

'That's not true!' Olivia sprang to her feet then, her pulses racing and her breasts heaving beneath the clinging folds of the caftan. 'How dare you come here and speak to me like this? It's not my fault that you and your father came to despise one another. That had nothing to do with me. I don't know why you split up and I don't care. But you have no right to accuse me of being greedy, when the minute your father's dead, you come here threatening to contest the will in your own favour!'

She had not meant to say that, but Alex surveyed her evident upheaval with unwilling admiration. 'So—it has claws, does it?' he mocked, as she struggled to control herself. 'And so vehement, too. When it obviously knows nothing about it.'

'I know enough,' declared Olivia tensely, not wanting to defend Henry, but unable to defend herself without doing so. 'I know something must have happened between you and your father to drive him to disown you. But that's in the past now——'

'No, it's not.' He stared at her contemptuously. 'You're here, aren't you? His grieving young widow! What's the matter, Livvy? finding it lonely?'

Olivia drew a deep breath. 'Please don't call me Livvy.'

'Why not? Is that what he used to call you?'

'No. No, your father always called me Olivia.'

'Okay, so I'll call you Liv,' he remarked carelessly. 'As I'm going to be around for a while, I guess we can dispense with formality. We are—related, after all.

Unless,' his dark eyes were disturbing, 'unless you'd like me to call you Mother.'

Olivia flushed. 'Don't be so ridiculous!'

'What's ridiculous? You are my—*step*mother, aren't you?'

Olivia's nervous tension was expanding not decreasing. This whole conversation was quite ludicrous, and yet it was all happening. 'I—I don't think that's relevant,' she said now, wishing she smoked so that she had something to do with her hands. They were fluttering about quite distractedly, and she knew he could not be unaware of her state of agitation. 'You didn't tell me where you were staying,' she said now. 'Do you have a base in London? What arrangements have you made?'

'None.' Now it was his turn to offer the negative. 'I didn't tell you where I was staying because I didn't know.'

Olivia's lips parted. 'You mean—you came right here from the airport?'

'Via Cosgrove's office, yes.'

'You've seen Adam?'

'Obviously.'

Olivia shook her head. 'But—how——'

'I hired a car at the airport,' he explained carelessly. 'I knew there was no chance I could get here in time for the funeral—my flight didn't land until four o'clock. So I made the diversion while I was in Chalcott. It's only an hour's drive, after all.'

'Yes.' Olivia was thinking hard. 'So—do you have any immediate plans?'

He studied the glowing tip of his cheroot. 'You tell me.'

Olivia hesitated. 'I suppose you need a bed for the night.'

'Yes.' He looked at her. 'Are you going to turn me out?'

Olivia caught her breath. 'Turn you out?' she echoed faintly, knowing as she did so that if she intended going through with her intentions, he should stay here. But after the things he had said, she was no longer certain of anything.

'I seem to remember you saying something about us being civilised,' he reminded her sarcastically.

'Yes, that's true. But——'

'But what?'

Olivia shook her head. She was getting out of her depth with this man. He was so totally different from what she had imagined, what she had expected. He disturbed her, he was an unpredictable quantity; and whatever she intended to do, she did not want him living in the same house.

'You said yourself, you—you and your father despised one another,' she began.

'No, you said that.'

Olivia pressed her palms together. 'You didn't disagree.'

'All right.' Alex tossed the remains of his cheroot into the fire behind him. 'So I didn't. But Henry's dead now, as you say, and there's just you and me, Liv. As Henry's surviving relatives, don't you think we should stick together?'

She knew he was baiting her. He didn't like her, and she was sure she didn't like him. It was strange how one's opinion could alter when faced with the realities of a situation. Earlier, she had half sympathised with Alex Gantry. She had been prepared to believe he was the innocent victim of his father's despotism. Now she was not so sure. Alex Gantry did not strike her as the kind of man who would care twopence for his father's feelings. He was hard, he was a predator; and no matter how he might excuse himself, she could not forgive his arrogant assumption that she had been cast in the same mould.

'What—what are your plans?' she ventured now, playing for time, needing a space to consider what she was going to do.

'Plans?' He was annoyingly obtuse. 'Why, some food and a good night's sleep. In that order,' he responded lazily, and Olivia's lips came together in a compressed white line.

'I mean—how long do you plan to stay in England? she exclaimed. 'You said you'd been working in Tsaba. How long do you intend to remain here? Surely your partner will expect you back.'

'My partner's dead,' he declared grimly, his eyes suddenly hard and uncompromising. 'And I have no immediate plans to return there. As it happens, I was planning to come to England quite soon, and it was a comparatively mild inconvenience to bring my trip forward.'

'You mean—you were coming to see your father?'

'We'll never know that now, will we?' he remarked flatly.

Olivia lifted her shoulders. 'I don't know what to suggest,' she was beginning stiffly, when a light tattoo on the panels of the door interrupted her and a moment later Mrs Winters appeared in the open doorway.

'I've had Cook make you a nice light omelette——' she started comfortingly, only to break off abruptly at the sight of the man standing squarely between herself and her mistress. Alex had turned his head at her entrance, so that Mrs Winters' first sight of him was in profile, and her mouth dropped open. Olivia, tense herself, was nevertheless aware of a certain tension about him as he confronted the housekeeper, and she realised with a pang, that he was apprehensive of her reaction. And why not? Olivia asked herself wryly. Mrs Winters had worked for his father for almost twenty years, and her loyalty might well not include a welcome for the son who had deserted Henry Gantry almost fifteen years ago.

Watching the housekeeper Olivia knew a sudden sympathy for her. This could not be easy, and the veined hands holding the tray shook a little as comprehension dawned. *'Alex?'* she mouthed, almost inaudibly. 'Master Alex, is that you?'

He moved then, taking the tray from her and setting it carelessly on one of the elegantly polished tables that flanked the armchair where he had been sitting. Then he smiled, and Olivia's heart took an unaccountable jolt. 'Don't you recognise me, Mrs Winters?' he demanded, his tone warm and teasing, and with a broken cry, the normally reserved Mrs Winters cast herself upon him.

'Oh, Master Alex,' she sobbed, clutching his shoulders, and gazing up into his face with unconcealed emotion. 'Oh, if only you'd come a week sooner!'

'I know, I know.' Alex allowed the housekeeper to enfold him in a convulsive embrace, but over the housekeeper's head, his eyes were mocking Olivia. Look, he seemed to be saying, you may have had it all your own way so far, but how do you feel about it now?

'Master Alex—that is, I mean—*Alex*—has just arrived from Africa, Mrs Winters,' she exclaimed, needing to exert her authority for no other reason than to reassure herself. 'He—I—perhaps you could prepare a room for him. And—and something to eat.'

'You're staying?' Without looking at Olivia, Mrs Winters addressed herself to Alex, and after exchanging another challenging look with Olivia, he nodded.

'It appears so,' he conceded, with infuriating coolness. 'Liv—Olivia—insists that it would be foolish for me to stay anywhere else.'

Olivia's gasp of indignation went unheard beneath the housekeeper's eager confirmation. 'Where else would you stay?' she exclaimed, drawing away from him with evident reluctance, and squeezing one of his hands be tween both of hers. 'If Mr Gantry was still alive——'

'But he's not,' Alex interrupted her firmly. 'It's better not to probe too deeply into old wounds, Mrs Winters. Who knows what would have happened if—if my father had still been alive?'

The housekeeper shook her head. 'He never forgave you, you know.'

'I know that.'

'I think he wanted to.'

'Do you?' Alex looked wry. 'You're very tactful, Mrs Winters.'

She sighed, gazing up at him with hungry eyes, almost as if she was afraid he might suddenly disappear again without notice. 'And you're much too thin,' she exclaimed, through trembling lips. 'Where on earth have you been all these years? What have you been doing? If only you'd written!'

Alex heaved a deep breath. 'Later, Mrs Winters,' he assured her gently. 'Right now, I could surely do with a bath and a change of clothes.'

'Of course.' Mrs Winters controlled herself and turned to Olivia now. 'With your permission, Mrs Gantry, I'll put Master Alex in his old room. It's the one overlooking the stables, and I think he'd like——'

'I know which room he used to occupy,' Olivia interposed briefly, her eyes the only indication of her angry indignation, and Mrs Winters, too bemused by Alex's reappearance to notice, smiled beneficently.

'Of course you do,' she beamed. Then she remembered the food cooling on its tray, and put an anxious hand to her throat. 'Would you like me to tell Cook you'll have a bit of dinner with Master Alex, instead of bothering with your omelette. I'm sure, now that you've got company——'

'The omelette is just fine,' replied Olivia crisply. 'I suggest you inform Cook of our unexpected guest's arrival, and she can prepare him a meal while he takes his bath. I—I shall be going straight to bed. I am rather—tired, after all.'

Mrs Winters' eyes widened. 'Oh, but——' She cast a troubled look in Alex's direction, and he, interpreting her anxiety, made an irritatingly complacent gesture.

'Don't worry,' he told her cheerfully. 'Olivia and I will have plenty of time to talk tomorrow. It's natural that she's feeling a little tired. Let's face it, it's been a long day, hasn't it, Liv?'

Olivia moved her head from side to side in an oddly confused way. Perhaps she was tired. Perhaps she was dreaming all this. Perhaps none of it was really happening! But she knew that she wasn't, and it was; and she was blankly aware of being outmanoeuvred at every turn.

Mrs Winters dragged her eyes away from Alex sufficiently long enough to give Olivia an encouraging smile. 'Then I'll go and attend to the arrangements,' she said, in the tone that falls midway between a statement and a question. And at Olivia's indifferent consent, she added: 'What about your luggage, Master Alex? Is it being sent on or what?'

'It's outside, actually. In the car I hired,' he declared casually, producing the keys.

'Then would you like me to get Murdoch——'

'Oh, no, that won't be necessary.' Alex pocketed the keys again. 'I'll get them myself.' He glanced at Olivia for a moment, and then went on: 'But perhaps you could arrange with the hire company to have the car collected tomorrow. I suppose while I'm here, you could lend me a car, couldn't you, Olivia?'

Olivia made another gesture which could have been acquiescence, and Mrs Winters's smile reappeared. 'Very well, then, I'll leave you for the moment.' She shook her head. 'Wait till Murdoch hears about this! He'll never believe it.'

'Oh, I'm sure he will,' Alex remarked in a low tone, as the housekeeper closed the door again behind her, and Olivia's resentment erupted into blazing anger.

'How dare you?' she demanded. 'How dare you? I did not insist that you stayed here, and as for lending you a car——'

'Yes?' His eyes were narrowed and wary.

'Oh—it's ludicrous!' Olivia thrust her hands forward, as if to ward off a physical presence. 'Whatever my feelings, you've inveigled your way in here—which reminds me: how did you get in? The gates are electrically operated, and we have a very efficient security system.'

'You forget, I used to live here,' Alex retorted blandly. 'And before you tell me the guard on the gate couldn't possibly remember me, I know. But it's amazing what the production of a passport will do, particularly when I explained how sorry I was not to have got here sooner. A son's grief still means something, Liv, even to hardbitten security guards.'

Olivia pursed her lips. 'I don't believe you're sorry at all. I think you timed your arrival perfectly!'

'Oh, *Mother*! How can you say that?'

His words mocked hers, and Olivia felt a helpless sense of impotence. Almost without volition, she was being backed further and further into a corner, and although she didn't want to fight him, he was making it impossible for her not to do so. What did he want? Why had he come here? And how long would he stay, if she did not make a stand?

With another bemused shake of her head, she moved then, intent on reaching the door and the comparative privacy of the hall beyond. But he moved too, stepping deliberately into her path, and she looked up at him angrily, incensed by his arrogance.

'Do you mind?' she exclaimed, her breathing quickening in concert with her emotions. 'I think we've said enough for one day, don't you? You're here—and thanks to Mrs Winters, you've acquired a certain respectability. But don't expect me to applaud your methods, because I won't. I don't know what your intentions are, but let me remind you, I am the mistress here, and don't you forget it!'

'Oh, I don't.' But he was mocking her again, his thin lips curling lazily as he surveyed her obvious frustration. 'You're the one who seems in danger of forgetting it. I mean, is this any way to treat a long-lost son?'

Olivia clenched her fists. 'Will you stop that!'

'And if I don't?'

'You're completely despicable, aren't you? I'm beginning to understand why Henry threw you out. I——'

'Correction, Henry did not throw me out,' Alex cut in harshly. 'I—walked out. Of my own free will.' He looked down at her contemptuously. 'He practically begged me to stay, do you know that?'

'Then you can't blame him, can you?' she exclaimed, seizing the opportunity he had given her, but he only shook his head.

'I don't,' he retorted coldly. 'But that doesn't stop me despising him, and what he did. I'm afraid your husband was no saint, Mrs Gantry.' He lifted a finger and before she could stop him, had brushed a sooty tendril from her cheek. 'Now ain't that a shame!'

Olivia flinched away from him, fumbling at the thread of hair with unsteady fingers, thrusting it back behind her ear, as if by doing so she would remove the unwanted touch of his skin. 'Don't do that!' she choked. 'Don't touch me! And please, get out of my way, before I——'

'Yes? Before you what? Throw a tantrum? Scream?'

He rucked up his jersey to tuck his thumbs into the low belt of his jeans. 'Dear me, I wonder what Mrs Winters would have to say about that? A nice piece of gossip to end the day with!'

Olivia took a deep breath. 'Why are you doing this?' she exclaimed tremulously. 'What do you want? I've said you can stay. Isn't that enough?'

He shrugged. 'Maybe I'm thinking that as we're what you might call—kissing kin, we should exchange something more than just goodnights.'

Olivia gasped. 'You must be crazy!'

'Why?'

He was a disturbing tormentor standing there, and in the warmth of the room, Olivia could not help but be aware of the raw male scent of his skin. It was not a sensation she was enjoying. She did not want to be aware of him, in any way; and her life to date had not led her to believe that she was likely to be affected by members of his sex. But the fact remained, she was disconcerted by his proximity, and uncomfortably conscious of his superior strength.

'Mr Gantry——'

'It was Alex a moment ago.'

'Alex, then——' She squeezed all her small store of composure into a tight ball. 'I think this conversation has gone far enough, don't you? If you'll just allow me to reach the door . . .'

'You haven't touched your supper,' he reminded her provokingly, and Olivia's shoulders sagged.

'I intend to take the tray up to my room,' she stated raggedly, although in fact she had only just remembered it. 'Alex, please, stop teasing me!'

'*Teasing!*' He made a stifled sound of derision, and before she could move, his hands gripped her waist, hard through the fine wool of the caftan. 'Teasing,' he said again, bending his head towards her. 'Oh, Liv, I'm not teasing!' and although she twisted her head away, his mouth sought and eventually imprisoned hers.

It was a cruel assault, made the more so by the savage way he forced her head round to his. His jaw was hard against her cheek, the roughness of his unshaven beard scraping her sensitive skin. His teeth bruised her lips as his own forced them apart, and the brutal pressure of his mouth on hers was a suffocating debasement.

Olivia tried to fight him off, but he was much too strong and much too determined to be thwarted by her puny efforts. Her hands pummelled uselessly at his back, but her breasts were crushed against his chest, and the rigid muscles of his legs were a solid barrier to any physical protest she tried to make.

His mouth silenced her verbal objections. Although sounds of resistance gurgled in her throat, she was powerless to help herself, and as the searching sensuality of his mouth continued to ravage her senses, new and disturbing sensations began to trouble her. His hands slid from her waist to her hips and evoked an uncontrollable response, and Olivia's defences crumbled. With the hungry demand of his lips softening to an unbearable intimacy, weakness enveloped her, and the hands which had only moments before been hammering at his shoulders were suddenly clutching the rough wool of his sweater.

'You—*bitch*!' he muttered suddenly against her lips, as his leg insinuated itself between hers, but the sound of his contemptuous voice, combined with the stirring pressure she could now feel against her stomach, brought Olivia to a horrifying awareness of what was happening.

'Oh, my God!' she choked, tearing her mouth from his. '*My God!*' and because he chose to let her go, she was able to drag herself away from him.

She wished the ground would open up and swallow

her when she saw the mocking gleam in his dark eyes, eyes that were almost black now as they raked her frozen revulsion. 'Poor Liv,' he taunted unkindly, making no attempt to hide his own arousal, 'you didn't find much satisfaction in your husband's bed, did you? You must have been desperate—'

Olivia's instinctive response rang quietly in the book-lined room, and her fingers stung horribly after impacting with his cheek. Gulping back a sob, she practically flew out of the door, and lifting the hem of the caftan she ran quickly up the stairs.

With the door of her room closed firmly behind her, she was forced to face the fact that his accusation had not been unjustified. Dear God, she thought disgustedly, she had behaved like the common slut he evidently thought her. How could she have allowed such a thing to happen? And today of all days! Henry was dead. Had Alex no respect? And how could she have played into his hands, and betrayed her own self-esteem? The tears she had not shed through these long and lonely hours spilled from her eyes and she wept for the realisation that she was not immune after all . . .

CHAPTER THREE

IT was barely eight o'clock when Olivia went downstairs. She had not slept, indeed, she had spent most of the night in the library, reading into the small hours after she was sure that Alex Gantry had gone to bed. And as soon as it was light, she had bathed and dressed, in black leather pants and a matching jerkin, and left her room once more. For once, she had no appreciation for her surroundings, and the thoughts which had occupied the long lonely hours of the night had left an unpleasant taste in her mouth. There were dark lines around her eyes, and she had fastened her hair at her nape with a strip of black leather. She looked like a hag, she thought dejectedly, finding nothing of beauty in her dark-fringed eyes and unsmiling mouth; but it was quite apt, she decided, because she felt like one.

The table in the dining room was laid for two, and for a moment Olivia wondered how Mrs Winters had known Francis was joining her for breakfast. But then the obvious explanation for those two place settings occurred to her, and her skin prickled unpleasantly in anticipation of the eventual encounter.

She had tormented her brain, trying to come to some decision regarding Alex Gantry. But the situation had been confused by what had happened the night before, and she could not entirely dissociate the man from the dilemma. It would have been easier if that disgusting scene had not taken place. But it had; and while she kept telling herself it had nothing to do with the issue, she was human—and it did!

It was strange, but she had imagined Alex Gantry

would be a weaker man. But he was Henry's son, after all, and how he must be congratulating himself for so cleverly insinuating himself back into the household. He had used Mrs Winters shamefully, exploiting her undoubted affection for him to his own ends, and creating an illusory image of his relationship with his step-mother. *His stepmother!* Olivia's skin crawled. He was not her stepson, she told herself fiercely; he was not, he *couldn't* be; but he was, and that made everything that had happened so much more shameful!

With her arms wrapped closely about herself, as if to ward off the evil thoughts that persisted in tormenting her, Olivia walked across to the windows. The dining room faced south, across the river, and the view had always been a source of delight to her. But not this morning. Not even the patches of blue, clearing in the overhanging skies, could lift the burden of despondency that seemed to be weighing her down, and even the sight of a pair of sparrows squabbling on the lawn could not lighten her mood.

'Oh, you're up, Mrs Gantry!'

Mrs Winters' surprised greeting brought Olivia round with a start, but she acknowledged the housekeeper's appearance with a faint smile.

'I couldn't sleep,' she said, perching on the edge of the window seat. 'It's a fine morning. Is it very cold?'

'Cold enough,' agreed Mrs Winters, viewing her mistress's pale face with some concern. 'Are you sure you should be up, Mrs Gantry? You're looking very tired.'

'Haggard is the word, Mrs Winters,' Olivia amended drily. 'I look haggard—I know it. It must be—delayed shock.'

Mrs Winters clicked her tongue. 'I knew yesterday was too much for you.'

'Oh, yes, you did. And it was.' Olivia's lips compressed. 'But don't worry, Mrs Winters, I'll survive.'

'If you say so, Mrs Gantry.' Mrs Winters sighed. 'But I do wish you'd take more care of yourself.'

Olivia made a barely audible sound of self-derision. 'Oh, so do I, Mrs Winters,' she agreed, and then, getting up from the window seat: 'By the way, Mr Kennedy is joining me for breakfast. Will you send him into Henry's study when he arrives? We'll have breakfast in there, if you don't mind.'

'Very well, Mrs Gantry.' But Mrs Winters was not pleased, and Olivia wondered if she was concerned for herself, or for Alex Gantry's sake. After all, it would be rather galling for him to come down and find himself eating in magnificent isolation. Still, he could always eat in his own room, she mused tautly. Somehow she did not think he was the type of man to allow any woman to get the better of him. Her lips tightened. She had not thought to ask whether he was married. Surely he could not be now or he would not have taken up her unwilling offer of accommodation. Unless he and his wife were separated; unless he was divorced.

'Will you have some coffee now?'

Mrs Winters was speaking again, and Olivia had to concentrate on what she was saying. 'What? Oh—oh, yes. That would be very nice, thank you.'

Francis arrived as she was drinking her second cup of strong black coffee. Murdoch showed him into the dining room, and Olivia got hastily to her feet to welcome him.

'I thought we'd have breakfast in Henry's study,' she said, after the preliminary greetings were over. 'If you have no objections, of course.'

'None whatsoever.' Francis was endearingly amenable.

'Oh, good.' Olivia offered a slight smile. 'Murdoch,

perhaps you'd tell Mrs Winters she can serve breakfast as soon as she likes.'

'Yes, Mrs Gantry.'

Murdoch inclined his greying head and left them, and rather nervously, Olivia led the way out of the dining room and along the wide, carpeted corridor to Henry's study.

This room had scarcely been touched since Henry's death. His desk was still littered with the papers and contracts he had been examining on the morning he had collapsed and been taken into hospital, and for all her studied indifference, Olivia could not deny the sudden dart of pain that pricked her heart. He had been her husband, after all, and six months could seem an awfully long time in retrospect.

Sweeping all the papers into her arms, she deposited them on the desk his secretary had used when she had been summoned to work at the house. Then, turning to Francis with a rather constrained expression, she indicated that he should sit down.

'You know this room so much better than I do,' she declared, taking Henry's chair at the opposite side of the desk. 'Did my husband do much work at home?'

Francis shrugged. 'Latterly, more than before.'

Olivia nodded. 'I imagine he came to depend on you completely.'

'Towards the end,' Francis agreed carefully. 'He was a very sick man, Mrs Gantry.'

'Yes, I know.' Olivia took a deep breath before resting her elbows on the table, and propping her chin on her knuckles. 'You were very loyal, Francis.'

'I did my job,' he maintained steadily.

'So——' She paused. 'What do you plan to do now?'

'Now?' He pulled a wry face. 'Why, to continue working for the company, I hope.'

'But without Henry, what will you do?'

Francis hesitated. 'I imagine you will be appointing someone as his successor, Mrs Gantry. No doubt that someone will need a personal assistant, someone who knows the business as well as I do.'

Olivia studied his serious face. 'Would you consider myself a suitable candidate?'

Francis stared at her, but before he could answer, there was a knock at the door. At Olivia's bidding, a red-faced maid pushed a trolley into the room, and there was no time for conversation as she laid a tablecloth across the desk, and set out silver-lidded dishes from the heated cabinet in the trolley. There was the delicious aroma of grilled bacon and fresh coffee, and the desk was soon transformed with plates of bone china and monogrammed knives and forks.

'Thank you, Julie.' Olivia dismissed the maid with a polite smile, and when the door had closed behind her, she offered Francis a choice of various fruits and cereals, grilled bacon, kidneys, eggs and sausages, and several different kinds of bread.

He refused everything but a slice of grilled bacon, and this, with her permission, he placed between two half slices of toast. 'I'm afraid I'm not used to a formal breakfast, Mrs Gantry,' he confessed, biting into his sandwich with evident relish nevertheless. 'I live in a service flat, as you probably know, and I generally don't bother with anything but coffee. And that, often out of a machine at the office.'

Olivia buttered a slice of toast for herself, and then, after pouring them both some coffee, she said: 'You're not married, are you, Francis? Haven't you ever felt tempted?'

His fair skin darkened with colour, and Olivia noticed how much more attractive he was in these less formal surroundings. Or perhaps she found any man an improvement on Alex Gantry, she thought tautly, as Francis gauged his reply.

'You don't buy something you can get for free, Mrs Gantry,' he said with a grimace. 'And until recently, I'd never met a woman I would be prepared to give up my freedom for.'

Olivia digested this. 'But now you have?'

'Yes.'

'Do I know her?'

Francis put down his sandwich. 'Mrs Gantry, what did you want to say to me?'

Olivia sighed, reluctant to abandon a subject that was so much more appealing than the one she had had in mind. 'I asked whether you considered I was capable of running the corporation,' she conceded slowly. 'Temporarily, of course.'

Francis frowned. 'I couldn't make that kind of judgment.'

'Why not? You know as much about the corporation as anyone, now that Henry's dead. And I should need your help.'

He shook his head. 'They'd never stand for it.'

'Who?'

'The other directors, Mrs Gantry. Your husband's directors. I'm sure they have a candidate of their own to put to you.'

'I'm sure they have, too.' Olivia caught her lower lip between her teeth. 'But—correct me if I'm wrong— I do have the majority shareholding, don't I?'

'Well—yes, but——' Francis lifted his shoulders. 'Mrs Gantry, there's no need for you to do this. You can rely——'

'Perhaps I don't want to rely on anyone,' she retorted swiftly. 'Except you, of course.'

Francis shook his head. 'You're not serious?'

'Why not?'

He sighed. 'Look, I know you were upset about the will. Cosgrove intimated as much. We had dinner together last night. He spoke in confidence, of course, but——'

Olivia pulled a wry face. 'I'm sure Adam Cosgrove is the soul of discretion.' She moistened her lips. 'Did he tell you he had seen Alex Gantry?'

'No!' Francis was evidently stunned. 'When did he see him? He didn't say anything to me. As I understood it, nobody knew where Alex was.'

'Well, apparently he did.' Olivia shrugged. 'He must have sent for him. He said he had tried to persuade Henry to alter his will in his favour.'

Francis looked astounded. 'You mean—he's here? In Chalcott?'

'I mean he's here—in this house,' declared Olivia flatly. 'But Alex Gantry is not under discussion right now. We—we'll come to that later.'

Francis made a bewildered gesture. 'I simply can't believe it! H.R. would never have allowed him in the house. Cosgrove knew that.'

'Yes. Well——' Olivia tried to sound philosophical, 'he is Henry's son, after all. I couldn't order him out of the house?'

'You could.' Francis warmed to his subject. 'Mrs Gantry, Alex Gantry was nothing but trouble to his father.'

Olivia bent her head. 'Francis, please! I've said I don't want to discuss it for the present. Can't we return to the matter in hand? That is why I invited you for breakfast.'

Francis relinquished his indignation with evident reluctance. 'I just wish I'd been here when he turned up, that's all,' he muttered. And then: 'Why do you really want to take over H.R.'s chair, Mrs Gantry?'

Olivia hesitated before replying: 'Because I intend

taking an active interest in the corporation's affairs.'

Francis was obviously mystified. 'I don't think H.R. would have expected that of you, Mrs Gantry,' he ventured, and Olivia felt a surge of mild hysteria.

'No, I don't suppose he would,' she agreed drily. 'But Henry's wishes are no longer relevant.'

Francis shook his head. 'Why are you telling me, Mrs Gantry?'

'I've told you—because I shall need your help. If you're willing. I promise you won't lose by it.'

Francis digested this, and then said quietly: 'But why me?'

'Because you were Henry's assistant. Because I feel I can trust you.'

Francis was obviously gratified, but he was too experienced in boardroom diplomacy to take that at its face value. 'I appreciate your confidence, Mrs Gantry,' he said, 'but I am sure there are others, more experienced than myself——'

'I doubt it.' Olivia's smile was wry. 'But all right. I want you working for me because you're the only member of Henry's staff I know well enough to confide in.' She paused. 'And because I think you don't entirely disapprove of me.'

Francis sighed. 'It's not my place to approve or disapprove, Mrs Gantry.'

'Oh, thank you. That's the stock answer, and you've made it.'

'It's not the stock answer.' Francis gazed at her frustratedly. 'I know these last six months haven't been easy for you.'

Olivia sighed. 'Why do you think I married Henry, Francis?' She paused, and then added: 'Don't bother to answer—I can see it in your face. You think it was for the money, don't you?'

'I think you're a very beautiful woman, Mrs Gantry,' replied Francis stiffly. 'And I don't blame you for using it to your advantage.'

Olivia sucked in her breath. 'Well, at least now you're being honest.' She shook her head. 'But I suppose you still think that for six months of marriage, to a man old enough to be my grandfather, I've come out of it rather well.'

Francis made a helpless gesture. 'Now you're putting words into my mouth, Mrs Gantry.'

'All right.' Olivia paused for a moment. 'I'll accept that you may have good reasons for your opinion. But, whatever you may think, I did not marry Henry for his money. If I had, we would not be having this conversation now.'

Francis looked at her. 'So—why did you marry him?'

'Naïve as it may sound, I married him for my mother's sake!' Olivia retorted, picking up the handle of a chased silver spoon, and digging her nail into its delicate tracery. 'It's a long story, Francis, and I won't bore you with it now. Sufficient to say that Henry Gantry destroyed my father's business, the business his father had founded over forty years before.'

'I see.' Francis nodded slowly. 'And your mother thought your marrying him would restore the family fortunes?'

'Not exactly.' Olivia was cynical. 'It's too late for that. As I said, it's a long story, and I admit, my mother played her part, too. She—she became infatuated with him, you see.'

'With H.R.?'

'Yes. Oh, this was years ago. I was just a baby. I knew nothing about it. But, apparently, she and Henry had—an affair.'

This part of the story was not easy for Olivia to relate, even though the participants were all dead now. Her

mother had not spared herself in its telling. She said she
had found her husband's new business acquaintance
fascinating, and his lean good looks and worldly air of
confidence had quite overshadowed her serious-minded,
hard-working husband.

Olivia could guess how it had been, particularly after
living with Henry herself for six months. He had been a
charming man, when it suited him, and Sophia Powell
hadn't stood a chance. Born in the East End of London,
to immigrant Italian parents, she had married Olivia's
father because her father had considered him a good
catch; but her passionate nature had been stifled by the
lack of gaiety and the shortage of money. Compared to
Henry's, her life had been dull and boring, and the only
excitement she had known was when he had begun to
pay attention to her.

It had all been over too quickly. Olivia's father had
learned Henry Gantry's intentions were not to put
money into his small chemical company to make it rich,
but so he had the power to close it down; and that,
combined with the discovery of his wife's infidelity, had
left him a broken man. Oh, Sophia had abandoned her
affair with Henry at once and spurned his protestations
of affection. For once in his life, Henry Gantry had
been thwarted. But the hatred their association had
inspired had fermented over the years, and when Mr
Powell died of a heart attack only eighteen months
later, the seeds of revenge had been sown in Sophia's
mind.

Even then nothing might have come of it, had it not
been for Henry himself. Olivia was just twenty-two,
straight out of university, and teaching at a com-
prehensive school in Croydon, when the arbiter of their
fate came back into their lives. She had not recognised
him, of course. He had just been a rather distinguished-
looking man who came to the flat one evening looking

for Mrs Powell. He had introduced himself as an old friend of her mother's, and as Mrs Powell had been in hospital at that time, recovering from one of her periodic bouts of depression, Olivia had not made the connection. She had actually enjoyed talking to him, and it wasn't until she went to the hospital and told her mother that she realised she had not got his name.

Her mother had been more astute. The description Olivia had been able to give, the Rolls-Royce with Forsyth at the wheel; they had been unmistakable clues to his identity; but when Olivia immediately exclaimed that she would tell him exactly what she thought of him next time he came around pretending to be a *friend* of her mother's, Sophia had become quite agitated. 'Let him come,' she had said, 'find out what he wants.' And when Henry had made his intentions known to Olivia, her mother had urged her to do as he asked.

He had come looking for Sophia, so he said, because he wanted a wife, because he knew he was dying, and because he wanted to make amends. When he discovered Sophia was ill, incurably ill, he had not hesitated in asking Olivia to marry him, and her mother had beseeched her to do it, naïvely thinking that when Henry was dead, everything would be hers.

Olivia had fought against it, but it had been an unequal battle. Mrs Powell might well have been sick, but her will was indomitable, and the chance to get even with Henry Gantry was one she could not bear to be denied. Besides, there was so much he could do for her mother: better hospitals, better treatment, better doctors. Mrs Powell had survived only four weeks of seeing her daughter as Henry Gantry's wife. Then she, too, had abandoned her hold on living, secure in the knowledge that justice had been served.

'So—your mother saw you as her revenge?' Francis

was asking now, and realising she had been staring into space for the past five minutes, Olivia gathered her composure.

'Something like that,' she agreed. 'And I suppose Henry saw her likeness in me. Either way, he married me. But I believe his real intention was to prevent Alex from inheriting.'

Francis frowned. 'Your husband was a connoisseur of beautiful women, Mrs Gantry. If all he had wanted was a beautiful wife, he could have taken his pick.'

Olivia half smiled. 'You're very good at your job, aren't you, Francis? Now I know why Henry thought so highly of you.'

Francis flushed. 'I mean it. Honestly, Mrs Gantry, I really think he cared about you. Perhaps he did love your mother. Perhaps she was wrong.'

'Perhaps.' But Olivia was sceptical. She had lived too long with her mother's memories to give that theory any credibility. 'Anyway,' she continued, 'I just wanted you to understand why I can't just sit back and live on his money.'

Francis stared at her. 'What do you hope to do? What do you hope to gain by it? You said—you wanted to take Henry's place, but only temporarily. Do you have another candidate in mind?'

Olivia hesitated. Then, with reluctant determination, she said: 'I'm considering appointing Alex Gantry as chairman.'

'What!' Francis could not have looked more astounded. 'Mrs Gantry, you can't mean it!'

Olivia shrugged, shivering a little in spite of herself. 'I said I was considering it,' she reminded him. 'That's why I shall need your advice.'

Francis thrust back his chair and got to his feet. 'I couldn't work with Alex Gantry. I'm sorry, Mrs Gantry, you'll have to find someone else.'

'Wait.' Olivia tried to sound composed, when in fact she was anything but. 'You can choose whether or not you work with him. You haven't heard my proposition.'

'You'll never be able to do it.' Francis' lips twisted. 'Your husband's fellow directors would resign first.'

'Would they?' Olivia considered this. 'Or perhaps, given time—and my influence—they might change their minds.'

'What do you mean?' Francis was suspicious.

'Well——' Olivia chose her words carefully, 'I've done quite a lot of reading since last night. The library's full of heavy tomes, dealing with every aspect of shares and share capital. I've read about stocks and dividend payments, and changes in capital structure. I even know the difference between voting and non-voting shares.'

'Mrs Gantry, what has this——'

'—to do with Alex Gantry?' Olivia cut in smoothly. 'Only to illustrate the fact that I know a little more now than I did. And as far as I can see, as the major shareholder, I can block every move the board intends to make!'

Francis made a choked sound. 'Why would you do that?'

Olivia shrugged. 'I'm a spoiled woman. I want my own way.'

Francis flung himself away from the table. 'I know that's not true,' he exclaimed. And then: 'Mrs Gantry—you know H.R. deliberately cut Alex out of his will.'

'I know it.'

'And this is your way of having your revenge?'

'If you say so.'

Francis expelled his breath disbelievingly. 'I think this

whole affair has been too much for you, Mrs Gantry.
Your husband's illness, the funeral—it's all been a
strain. I think you need a break—a holiday. Yes, that's
it, a holiday. Somewhere far away from here, somewhere
warm and relaxing, and completely free of responsibilities——'

'Like a sanatorium?' suggested Olivia drily, getting to
her feet. 'Are you suggesting Henry's death has un-
balanced me, Francis?'

'I'm suggesting you should think again, Mrs Gantry.'

'Why?'

Francis spread his hands. 'Alex Gantry is a loser, Mrs
Gantry. He always was, and he always will be. For
God's sake, why give him something he doesn't deserve? If you do what you say you're going to do, you
can run the corporation into the ground without his
help!'

Olivia's lips parted. 'Run the corporation into the
ground?' she echoed, and Francis looked discomfited.

'Perhaps,' he muttered unwillingly, and she smiled.

'Poor Francis,' she said. 'You have been indiscreet.
But are you really prepared to take your chances with
the other directors, when I'm prepared to offer you a
quarter of a million pounds for your block of shares.'

'A quarter of a million!'

Francis' mouth dropped open, but his hushed echo
of her words was abruptly superseded by the opening of
the study door. They both stood, almost guiltily, staring
at the intruder, but Alex Gantry's face showed nothing
but narrow-eyed amusement as he advanced into the
room.

'Well, well,' he remarked lazily. 'What have we here?'
His dark eyes flickered mockingly over Olivia's face
before they turned to examine the covered dishes still
standing on the desk. 'Bangers and bacon, as I live and
breathe,' he added, lifting one of the silver lids and

helping himself to a sausage. 'Hmm, you don't know how much I've looked forward to a proper English breakfast!'

Francis exchanged a charged look with Olivia, and realising she should take the initiative, she forced herself to make the introduction: 'You know Henry's son, don't you, Francis?' she asked, unable to keep the annoying tremor out of her voice as Alex turned to look at her. 'Alex—you remember Francis Kennedy, I'm sure. Your father's personal assistant?'

The two men shook hands, Alex hastily depositing the remains of the sausage in his mouth, and borrowing Olivia's napkin to wipe his hands before making the salutation. He was looking more civilised this morning, she noticed with some misgivings. He had shaved, for one thing, and brushed the smooth lick of hair, that still persisted in straying over his forehead. His navy corded jeans were tight-fitting, but reputable, and his cream silk shirt looked as expensive as one of Henry's. But there was still that air of arrogant masculinity about him, that acted like an abrasive on Olivia's raw senses, and in spite of what Francis had said, she did not think he looked like a loser.

'You're an early riser, Kennedy.' He addressed the other man casually, unperturbed by Francis' taut expression. 'I hope I'm not interrupting anything important. I just came to wish my stepmama good morning.'

Olivia could feel the tiny hairs on the back of her neck rising in angry protest at this deliberate provocation, and Francis looked as if he was controlling his feelings with difficulty.

'What a surprise to see you back here again, Gantry,' he said caustically. 'You've been away for such a long time, we all thought you were dead.'

'And how much easier it would have been for all of

you if I was,' remarked Alex without aggravation. 'But then I'd never have met this charming stepmother of mine, and that would have been a shame!'

'Alex, please——' Olivia's entreating whisper fell on deaf ears, as he sauntered round the desk to where she was standing her hands clenched stiffly at her sides.

'Good morning, Liv,' he greeted her sardonically, and while she stood there in frozen immobility, he bent towards her and deposited an insolent kiss on the vulnerable parting of her lips.

CHAPTER FOUR

FRANCIS, watching them, looked thunderstruck, and Olivia wondered with a pang whether he imagined she and Alex had planned this whole affair. It was not an unreasonable supposition. Stranger things had happened in the pursuit of wealth, and he could easily be forgiven for speculating which of the Gantry's she had known first: the father, or the son.

But he couldn't think that, he *mustn't* think that, she thought in horror, and her hand itched to wipe the derisive expression from Alex's mocking face. He was contemptible, she thought disgustedly, *evil*, a devil, who had every intention of robbing her of any self-respect.

With a moan of distaste she recoiled from him, and his lips barely brushed hers. But the damage was done, and although she pushed him away from her, the way he rocked back on his heels seemed to imply an inconsistency common to females.

'Don't do that!' she hissed, her eyes sparkling with green fire, but Alex was unashamed.

'I couldn't resist it,' he responded, turning to Francis and spreading his hands. 'Women!' he added infuriatingly. 'They're so damned unpredictable!'

'Francis——' Olivia stepped forward, needing to re-establish her contact with the other man. 'We—er—we obviously can't continue our discussions now. I wonder if we could meet later.'

'Why don't you invite him for dinner?' Alex suggested blandly, pushing his hands into the pockets of his pants. 'I'm sure Mrs Winters will be happy to have guests in the house again. There can't have been much for her to do lately.'

'Will you be quiet?' Olivia did not try to hide her frustration now, and she could feel a pulse racing in her temples as she fought to keep control of the situation.

'I'll be out myself,' Alex went on unconcernedly. 'I've got one or two friends I want to look up, and I just thought——'

'Do you have any friends, Gantry?' Francis' nostrils flared. 'I don't know of any.'

'Oh, I imagine I have as many as you do, Kennedy,' Alex countered pleasantly. 'And at least I know who mine are.'

'Francis!' Olivia was getting desperate. 'About tonight——'

'I'm afraid I can't.' Francis spoke stiffly, and she couldn't tell from his expression what was going on in his mind.

'Are you sure?' she persisted, imploring him with her eyes, and as if taking pity on her, he offered an explanation.

'It's a dinner, I'm obliged to attend,' he told her quietly. 'I'm sorry, but I can't get out of it.'

'Now isn't that a shame!' Alex was almost insolent, perching on the edge of the desk, his long legs splayed in front of him. 'It looks like I'll have to abandon my plans and keep you company, Liv.'

'Don't bother!' She almost spat the words at him, and as if deciding that there was nothing to be gained by hanging on here, Francis moved towards the door.

'I've got to go, Mrs Gantry,' he said, checking his tie in a revealingly nervous gesture. 'I suggest you give me a ring at the office. We can make some other arrangement.'

'Yes. Yes, all right, I'll do that.' Olivia nodded her head jerkily. 'I'm sorry about this, Francis.'

'Don't worry about it——'

'No, don't worry about it,' seconded Alex provokingly. 'You don't have to apologise, Liv. Henry never
apologised for anything.'

'Will you shut up?'

Olivia's nerves were stretched to screaming pitch, and
she was trembling so badly she had real misgivings about
trusting her legs at all. But she had to get away from
Alex Gantry's taunting voice, and when Francis pulled
the door wide she hurried after him, tucking her hand
through his sleeve as they ascended the steps to the
upper hall.

'I'll see you later in the week then,' she ventured, as
they walked towards the outer door, but Murdoch appeared, to hand Francis his overcoat, and any private conversation they might have had was abruptly curtailed.

'Yes, later in the week,' he agreed, sliding his arms
into the coat the butler was holding. Then, as if in reassurance, he added: 'Be careful, Mrs Gantry. I don't
want you to get hurt.'

'Nor do I, Francis,' murmured Olivia ruefully, and
relinquished the hand he had offered reluctantly, as if
abandoning a lifeline.

'The representative of the car hire firm arrived a few
minutes ago, to take possession of Master Alex's
vehicle,' Murdoch informed her as he closed the door. 'I
gave him the keys, as you instructed.'

'As I instructed?' echoed Olivia blankly, and then saw
Alex watching them at the foot of the staircase she had
just mounted. His sardonic expression invited her to
challenge him, but remembering how skilfully he could
confound her, she merely made a sign of assent and
turned towards the upper staircase.

'Hey—wait!' he called then, taking the steps two at a
time, and because Murdoch was still within earshot
Olivia had to obey, or risk the kind of gossip she

most wanted to avoid.

'What do you want?' she demanded, her tone as icy as her face, and he halted in front of her, his dark eyes assessing.

'Is this any way to treat a guest?' he protested, adopting a wounded expression. 'The least you can do is join me for breakfast.'

'I've had breakfast,' pointed out Olivia shortly, but Alex only shrugged.

'I haven't,' he responded. 'And you didn't eat much. I guess that creep Kennedy ruined your appetite.'

'If anyone ruined my appetite, it was you,' Olivia snapped angrily. 'How dare you behave as if you owned me! I don't know what Francis thought, but I can imagine, and I may have the greatest difficulty in persuading him otherwise.'

'Why try?' Alex surveyed her insolently. 'Is his good opinion so important to you?'

'His opinion is important because he happens to care what happens to me,' she retorted coldly.

'I'll bet he does.' Alex was laconic. 'You're a very powerful lady, and he's not likely to forget it.'

'That's not what I meant!' Olivia was incensed.

'Okay.' Alex raised a conciliatory hand. We'll agree to disagree, shall we? How about some breakfast?'

'I'm not hungry.'

'A walk, then.'

'A walk?' Olivia stared at him incredulously. 'Do you honestly think I'd go for a walk with you?'

'I think you might,' he conceded, tucking his hands into the hip pockets of his pants. 'I mean—you don't want to create the wrong impression, do you? Not if I'm staying here. We're—stepmother and stepson; we're related; and unless you plan to throw me out, you'd better get used to the fact.'

Olivia felt a quiver of distaste sweep over her at his

words. But she could not deny their veracity. Unless she wanted to make an enemy of him, she had to play the game his way, at least until she had spoken to Francis again.

'I think you're despicable,' she said now, wrapping her arms about herself protectively. 'And I want you to know, if you ever try anything like you tried last night again, I will scream, and be damned to you!'

'Okay.' Alex took the admonition indifferently. 'So get your coat. I think we could both use some fresh air.'

Olivia stared at him helplessly. His arrogance was unbelievable! Did he really expect her to walk with him after this?

'You'd better put on some rubber boots,' he added over his shoulder, as he mounted the stairs to the upper floor. 'As I recall it, the ground beside the river is pretty marshy, and after last night's rain, it will probably be quite muddy.'

Olivia expelled her breath on an aggravated sigh. She would not go walking with him, she thought, she would not! But then the prospect of spending the next hour or so wondering what she was going to do overrode her objections, and tugging angrily at an unruly tendril of hair, she unwillingly climbed the stairs after him.

Mary was in her room, tidying the bed she had occupied so briefly the night before. She looked round expectantly as Olivia came into the room, and her expression revealed she knew what had happened.

'Fancy,' she exclaimed, 'Mr Gantry's son turning up like that out of the blue! You could have knocked me down with a feather. And his father scarcely cold in his grave, too, if you'll pardon the expression.'

Olivia acknowledged the girl's excited chatter with a wry grimace. But she made no response, crossing the bedroom to her dressing room and rummaging about in the bottom of the closet for the rubber wellingtons she had worn when she and Henry had paid a visit to the site of a new factory.

'Can I help you, Mrs Gantry?'

Mary's questioning face appeared in the doorway, and Olivia, finding what she had been looking for, got to her feet. 'It's all right, Mary,' she said, waving the boots in the air. 'I only wanted these. I—er—I'm going for a walk, and I believe the grass is muddy.'

Mary glanced towards the windows, observing the watery sunshine with some misgivings. 'It isn't much of a day for walking, Mrs Gantry,' she remarked, pressing her lips together half impatiently when Olivia refused her offer of assistance. 'You want to wrap up warm now. Mrs Winters said you looked peaky, and I agree with her.'

Olivia sighed. 'I'm perfectly all right, Mary. I—just slept rather badly, that's all.'

'Mr Murdoch said he saw the light on in the library, long after midnight,' declared Mary doggedly. 'You really ought to get your sleep, Mrs Gantry. We don't want you looking all eyes and cheekbones, now that Master Alex is here.'

Olivia turned away, using the excuse of finding a coat to wear to avoid Mary's searching stare. 'I don't think my appearance will make the slightest bit of difference, Mary,' she replied, pulling out a warm pigskin jacket. 'This will do, I think. Now, where are those sheepskin mittens?'

'He's very handsome, so I hear,' Mary persisted, as she riffled through a drawer and came up with the errant mittens. 'All brown and tanned with the sun, and streaky fair hair, just like Robert Redford.'

'Oh, really, Mary!' Olivia practically snatched the mittens from her and marched towards the door. 'Alex Gantry is nothing like Robert Redford! So you can stop behaving as if he was some kind of film star.'

Mary shrugged, by no means abashed. 'Well, he's certainly brought a bit of excitement into your life, Mrs Gantry,' she exclaimed. 'I mean, who would have expected Mr Gantry's son to come back after fifteen years!' She grimaced. 'And to find he has a stepmother younger than he is! That's a turn-up for the book.'

'I'd be grateful if you wouldn't indulge in gossip about my relationship to—to Mr Gantry.' Olivia told her stiffly, hovering by the door. 'I realise his arrival must have aroused some speculation, but this is his home, after all, and—and it's just unfortunate that he came too late to see his father.'

'Of course, Mrs Gantry.' Mary looked the soul of discretion, but Olivia knew better than to believe everything she said. The whole affair couldn't be anything less than a nine days' wonder among the members of the household staff, and she could only hope her patience was equal to theirs.

Alex was waiting for her downstairs, pacing restlessly about the hall, showing little interest in his father's painting collection. He, too, was wearing boots over his dark slacks, but the jerkin he had adopted would provide scant protection against the weather.

Olivia hesitated, and then, reaching the foot of the stairs, she said shortly: 'Don't you have a warmer jacket? Or an overcoat? The temperature's not much above freezing, and I don't suppose you want to catch a chill.'

Alex lifted his shoulders carelessly. 'I didn't know you cared,' he remarked mockingly, and then, as if feeling some remorse for her indignation, he added: 'I don't have a warmer jacket. We didn't go in much for warm jackets in Gstango. But when I get to the shops, I'll bear what you say in mind.'

Olivia sighed, and then, with an almost sixth sense of someone else's presence, she glanced behind her. Mary was standing at the top of the stairs, her face alight with curiosity, which quickly turned to embarrassment when she met her mistress's angry stare.

'Did you want something, Mary?' Olivia enquired pointedly, keeping her temper on a tight rein, and the other girl made an awkward gesture.

'I—er—I was just coming downstairs, Mrs Gantry,' she offered, as Alex turned appraising eyes in her direction. 'I'm sorry, I'm sure. I didn't mean to intrude.'

Olivia squeezed the sheepskin mittens between her fingers, and then, ignoring Alex's evident amusement, she said: 'Well, you can do something for me instead. Go into my husband—go into Mr Gantry's room, and fetch down a sheepskin jacket. There are several there. Any one will do. And hurry.'

'Yes, Mrs Gantry.'

Mary's hesitation was hardly perceptible, but after she had gone, Alex surveyed Olivia wryly. 'So I'm to put on my father's jacket, am I? Aren't you afraid I might find it fits?'

The double entendre was unmistakable, but Olivia refused to be disconcerted. 'Would that be so unusual?' she suggested. 'If it did? You are your father's son, aren't you? Apart from the fact that you're a little taller than he was, you're of a similar build.'

Alex's eyes narrowed. 'You're very generous,' he drawled, and Olivia looked confused.

'Generous?' she echoed. 'I'm afraid I——'

'Accepting the fact that I fit my father's shoes so much better than you do,' he explained mockingly. 'Doesn't it trouble you that I might not want to take them off?'

Thinking of what she planned to do, Olivia drew a deep breath: 'Perhaps—perhaps I won't ask you to,' she ventured softly, and then gulped in dismay when Alex's hands fastened on her shoulders. They were strong hands, hard and calloused, as she had discovered the night before, and even through the thick skin of her coat they hurt!

'Don't play games with me!' he grated, and for a moment she was too stunned to answer him. 'I was only trying you out last night, *Mrs* Gantry. I was interested to see how far you would go. Well, we both know what happened, don't we, and as far as I'm concerned you deserve everything that's coming to you!'

'I don't know what you mean!'

Olivia dragged herself away from him, trembling with a mixture of emotions that were not expelled by the contemptuous expression on his face. 'Oh, you know,' he told her harshly. 'You married Henry to get your hands on all this, and now you find it's not enough; you need something more!'

'You're crazy——'

'Am I?' He stepped close to her again, and it was all she could do not to back away from him. 'You're a sexy lady, Liv, but you'll never know now whether they want you—or your money! What do you want from me, I wonder? Reassurance?'

'I want nothing from you!' Olivia spat the words, but Alex was unrepentant.

'I can't believe that, Liv. You're scared of me, for some reason.' He shook his head. 'But don't push me too far, stepmother dear, or I may just decide to take you up on your most generous offer, and that would be disastrous for both of us!'

Olivia pressed her hands to her middle, trying to dispel the raw feeling inside her, and as she did so, Mary came down the stairs with the sheepskin jacket. Alex moved away from her, and she doubted the girl had noticed how close they had been a few moments before, but Mary had sharp eyes, and she was astute enough to realise there had to be a reason for her mistress's hectically-flushed cheeks. Olivia could imagine the gossip that would ensue in the kitchen after this little fiasco, and guessed that Mary would enjoy her unexpected notoriety.

'Will this coat do, Mrs Gantry?' she asked, offering a thigh-length jacket with a soft suede exterior, and Olivia nodded gauntly as Alex took it from the maid.

'This is exactly what I need, Mary,' he exclaimed, taking off his jacket before sliding his arms into the sleeves of the warm sheepskin. 'Thank you for getting it for me.' He smiled disarmingly. 'I think Mrs Gantry is concerned about my health.'

'Well, it is a cold morning, sir,' Mary assured him, flattered by his attention, and Olivia turned away in disgust. She did not know how he could behave so courteously to the maid after his insulting behaviour to her, and although she was trying to be objective, her own feelings were hardening.

'Shall we go?'

Alex's breath fanned her cheek, and she glanced round half-guiltily to find Mary had gone.

'Are you sure you want me to come with you?' she asked, meeting his dark eyes with enforced indifference. 'I mean—I should have thought you would rather explore the private places of your youth without my tainted presence!'

His brows arched. 'The lady has a sense of humour.'

'No. I would simply prefer to avoid any further outbursts like the last one.'

'Why?' He shrugged. 'Don't you like the truth?'

'No more than you do, apparently,' retorted Olivia coldly. 'You're the prodigal, Mr Gantry, not me. Too bad all the fatted calves are dead!'

'What a sharp little tongue you have, stepmother!' he taunted grimly, and then, as if growing tired of the argument, he put one hand on her shoulder and guided her towards the door. 'Come on. The air's got to be fresher outside than in this mausoleum.'

'We go out through the sun lounge,' Olivia was forced to remind him, and she thought for a moment he looked quite confused. But then, with an indifferent shrug of his shoulders, he allowed her to lead the way, and they descended the stairs again that gave access to the back of the house.

The terrace that ran across the rear of the building gave on to a mosaic-tiled patio, with an elegantly-shaped swimming pool empty now, forming a centrepiece. There were poolside cabanas, half hidden by trellises, and shallow steps leading down to a rose garden. The whole area looked rather forlorn at this time of year, but when Olivia had first seen it, it had been a riot of colour.

Alex stood for a few moments on the terrace, his breath misting in the chilly air, surveying the lawns beyond the rose garden, and the hedge of tall poplars that grew at the side of the house. His eyes dipped over a sloping paddock, fenced about with white rails, to the marshy meadow beside the river, and then lifted again over the undulating farmland he could see across the swiftly-flowing water.

'That's Gantry land; too, isn't it?' he remarked, pointing towards a field where a flock of ewes and their lambs were gathered together for warmth.

'Yes.' Olivia followed his gaze. 'When the farms came on the market, your father bought them.'

Alex made a sound deep in his throat. 'He certainly had a head for business, didn't he? I wonder what he paid for them in those days. The land must be worth a hell of a lot more today.'

'I suppose so.' Olivia's tone was flat now. 'Shall we go on?'

They followed the path that led between lawns and flower borders, sadly neglected now, until they reached the paddock. Olivia looked at Alex, and then swung herself up on to the rail, swinging her leg over and jumping down into the spongy turf beyond. There was a gate, but she had seldom used it, and as she generally walked alone, she was used to climbing fences.

'Is this how you keep slim?' asked Alex, vaulting over the fence and joining her in the paddock.

'I enjoy walking,' Olivia conceded. 'I suppose you're used to plenty of exercise.'

'Well, it isn't a cushioned existence,' he admitted drily. 'But I get most of my exercise trying to persuade a lethargic work-force it's in their best interests as well as mine to increase productivity.'

Olivia glanced his way. 'You mean the men who work in your mine?'

'I do.'

She paused. 'What kind of mine is it?'

'Oh——' he hesitated, 'we quarry mineral ore in large quantities. Unfortunately, valuable minerals are present in such small amounts, the cost of the work involved can outweigh its value.'

'I see.' Olivia was interested in spite of herself. 'I think I read something like that about oil in Alaska. But they're building a pipeline now, aren't they?'

'That's because oil has become so expensive,' replied Alex easily. 'What was once an unreasonable proposition is now feasible, and the oil companies are the last people to sit on a good idea.'

'You sound as if you know about oil,' commented Olivia quietly. 'Have you ever worked for an oil company?'

'Me?' Alex looked at her strangely. 'Hell, no. Didn't my father tell you! I'm not interested in chemicals.'

Olivia shrugged. 'So—do you like living in Africa?' she asked, not wanting to dwell on such a controversial subject. 'Where was it you said you lived? Tsaba? Is that a very big country?'

'No.' Alex scuffed his boot in the grass. 'Quite a small

one, actually. But the people are friendly, and communications are good.'

They had reached the boundary of the paddock, and Olivia stopped and rested her arms on the fence. 'How long have you lived in Africa?' she asked. 'I only know you left here in 1967, and that your father hadn't seen you since.'

Alex propped his elbows on the rail beside her, and studied the view. Because he wasn't looking at her, Olivia felt quite at liberty to look at him, and she noticed the lighter tones of the skin around his eyes where he had screwed them up against a powerful sun. He had very brown skin, unusual with such ash-fair hair, his brows firm and clearly marked, his lashes thick and short and bleached at the tips. His nose was straight above a well-formed upper lip, the lower lip fuller, and definitely sensuous. He was not handsome, she thought critically, but he was attractive, and with his age and experience she doubted she was the first female to make that comparison.

She was so absorbed with her thoughts, she was unaware he had turned to look at her, and she started violently when he said: 'Why did you marry Henry, Liv? I can't believe he was the only pebble on your stretch of the beach.'

'If that means what I think it means, then my answer should be that there aren't too many men like your father around,' she retorted, giving him the benefit of her profile. She put her hands on the rail. 'Shall we go down to the river? There are some wild geese nesting in the reeds. If you're very lucky, you may catch sight of them.'

'Cool it!' Alex's hard fingers compelled her acquiescence, curving around her forearm, and preventing her from rising. 'What I meant was—you're a good-looking woman: you can't have been that desperate for a meal-ticket!'

'How charmingly you put it!' Olivia exclaimed, her breathing quickening instinctively. 'I know you won't believe this, but my reasons for marrying your father had little to do with inheriting his estate!'

Alex considered her indignant face for a moment, then he said harshly; 'You're right, I don't believe it.'

'Suit yourself.'

Olivia was abrupt, and his immediate response was to subject her to an unnerving stare. 'You're not telling me you fell in love with the old man, are you?' he demanded, but there was an element of mild incredulity in his tones just the same, as if he wasn't completely certain.

'No.' Olivia refused to give him that satisfaction, even though it might have been easier for her. 'No, I didn't love him. As a matter of fact, I hated him! Now—shall we continue?'

She did find some satisfaction in Alex's stunned reaction, but she was intelligent enough to realise that once his initial shock was over, she could expect a much more violent response. It might be perfectly satisfactory for him to express criticism of his father; hearing criticism from another quarter was an entirely different thing.

But once again he confounded her, releasing her wrist and climbing over the fence into the marshy meadow beyond. He waited for her to join him, and with some misgivings she did so, avoiding the hand he offered to assist her and dropping down cautiously on to the swampy grass.

'Tell me,' he said, as they squelched down the slope towards the river, 'what did you do before you got married? What were you, a model or something? Or simply somebody's secretary?'

'What does it matter?' Olivia pushed her hands into the pockets of her coat. 'Do you think it looks like snow? I don't know how those lambs survive in this climate.'

'They wear coats, like this one,' remarked Alex laconically, picking up a stone and sending it flying across the water in a series of arches. 'Ducks and drakes—did you used to play that when you were a little girl?'

Olivia shook her head. 'I lived in London all my life until I got married. There weren't many places where we could play. Just in the square below the flats, and occasionally my mother took me to the park. But she didn't allow me to go there alone, or with the other children.' She sighed, not really thinking how revealing her words might be. 'She was very protective.'

'Protective—or possessive?' Alex probed, watching her closely, and Olivia chided her careless tongue for telling him so much.

'She's dead now anyway,' she said, hoping that would be an end of it. She gestured towards the wooden structure, some way farther along the riverbank. 'Do you remember the boathouse? Your father said it was once occupied, but not in recent years.'

'No.' Alex surveyed the creosoted exterior of the building with brooding eyes. 'And yes, I remember it. How could I forget?'

Olivia looked quickly at him. 'What do you mean? What significance does it have for you? Was it your boat he kept there? I suppose he sold it after you left.'

'The boat sank,' declared Alex flatly, turning abruptly away. 'Let's go back to the house, shall we? I've got some telephone calls to make.'

Olivia was puzzled, but she could not ask him to explain. Obviously whatever the boathouse meant to him had something to do with his past relationship with his father, and she was loath to rekindle the hostility that that association bred. For almost an hour they had remained civil with one another, which was something of a record, but all the same she wished she knew what he was thinking.

Back at the house, he was his old objectionable self, flinging his father's jacket on to the chest in the hall and striding with abominable arrogance down to his father's study.

'You don't mind if I make my calls in there, do you?' he asked Olivia, as she hovered doubtfully on the upper level, her hands still pressed deeply into the pockets of her coat. His tone was provoking, willing her to challenge him, but Olivia squashed her indignation and replied: 'Why not?'

'Don't you want to know who I'm going to ring?' he persisted, mocking her indifference. 'Aren't you at all perturbed that I might find some allies, some faces on the board who found the spectacle of Henry Gantry marrying a girl scarcely out of her teens totally out of character? The old man must have been senile. And with the right backing, it might be possible to prove it!'

'It would be totally untrue!' Olivia was stung into retaliation. 'Your father had complete possession of his faculties, right up until the end.' Her face twisted. 'I don't know how you can suggest such a thing! He was your father!'

Alex's eyes narrowed. 'Have I touched a raw nerve? It seems to me, for someone who professed only a few minutes ago that she hated him, you're remarkably quick to come to his defence.'

Olivia's teeth jarred together. 'And you're completely without sensitivity! My God, he was only buried yesterday. Can't you at least show a little respect!'

Alex shrugged. 'Why should I? He never showed any respect for anyone, least of all me. Unless you know different.'

Olivia turned towards the stairs. In every argument she came out the loser, and every time she came near to telling him what she wanted to do, he forced her back into a defensive position.

'By the way,' Alex lifted one foot to the second step, resting one arm across his knee, 'you didn't tell me what car I could use, and as I intend to go out after I've made my calls, I'd like a firm decision.'

Olivia gasped. 'I didn't tell you because I haven't given the matter any thought,' she retorted. 'I suggest you get a car of your own. There are plenty of garages in Chalcott.'

'Okay.'

Alex dropped his foot again and stood looking up at her, his dark eyes enigmatic between the lowering thickness of his lashes. Olivia, delaying in spite of herself, could not prevent an unwelcome awareness of him, a conscious response to his sexuality, that was wholly instinctive. He really was the most disturbing man she had ever known, and the realisation that she was attracted to him hit her like a blow to her solar plexus. Dear God, she thought, swinging round on her heels and groping for the reassuring rail of the banister, she must be out of her mind! Either that or, as he had accused her, desperate for attention. But one thing was certain, she thought, shivering with a sudden chill, whatever her hang-ups, he was the one man she could never have.

CHAPTER FIVE

'You have to be crazy, Mrs Gantry!'

Olivia was sitting in Francis Kennedy's office on the twenty-second floor of the Gantry building, and from her chair she had a magnificent view of the city spread out below her. The only floor above this one was the penthouse apartment, where Henry used to entertain visiting business associates, and where he occasionally held parties for his senior office staff.

Henry's office was the one adjoining Francis', a large square panelled room, with a huge portrait of Henry himself hung above the mantel. Like this room, it had wide windows overlooking Curzon Street with Hyde Park beyond, but Olivia still felt vaguely intimidated by its air of stern solemnity.

Francis' office was different. It was lighter, for one thing, without the heavy oak panels, and the walls were hung with prints of old Aston Martins and Lanchesters, and a Model T Ford, reflecting Francis' interest in vintage cars.

But right now, Francis' face was as stern and as solemn as the walls of Henry Gantry's office. It was just a week since the funeral, a week since Alex Gantry had burst into her life, and Olivia wished she felt more capable of upholding her decision.

It hadn't helped to go down with a severe cold two days after Alex's arrival. She guessed she had contracted the cold standing by the graveside, and remembering how chilled she had felt, it was hardly surprising. Nevertheless, it was unusual for something as trivial as a cold to confine her to her room for several days, and she could only assume that Mrs Winters had been right, and that she had taken too little rest in recent weeks.

She refused to admit that Alex's hostility had been the reason for her exhaustion. His presence had complicated the situation, but she would have to learn to live with it. She refused to believe that her body's frailty could in any way be contributable to the weak moment when she had experienced that unwilling attraction towards him. It had been a fleeting thing, she had told herself, an acknowledgement of his undoubted strength and virility. As a person, she had only contempt for his callousness and his arrogance, and there were times, as now, when she half wished she had never devised this method of overruling her husband's last wishes.

Not that she had seen much of Alex since their argument over the cars. According to Mary, whose nose for gossip she had shamefully exploited, Master Alex had spent little time in the house, but there had been several calls for him, and it was these that had interested Olivia most. It had been a little chastening to find that people like Barry Freeman and Sean Barrett had returned his calls, but she had consoled herself with the reassurance that both these men must have known him since he was born. It was only natural that they might have some lingering affection for Henry Gantry's son, but she did not think either of them would look kindly on a plan to dishonour Henry's name.

There had been two calls from a woman who called herself Missy. Mary had been quite conspiratorial when relating this information to Olivia. 'It was so funny,' she exclaimed, stifling a giggle, 'I answered the phone, you see, because I was in the hall at the time, and this woman said in this awfully sexy voice: 'Could I speak to Mr Gantry, please?'

'So?' Olivia had been impatient. 'What was funny about that?'

'Well,' Mary warmed to her story, 'I said Mr Gantry wasn't here right now, and she said: "Oh, damn!" or something like that, and then she said: "Tell Leon I called!" I mean—imagine! She must have so many boy-friends, she even gets their names mixed up!'

Olivia had acknowledged this rather dubiously, but afterwards she had come to the conclusion that Leon could be a derivation of Alexander. Who knew what names a woman might call her lover in the heat of passion? she had reflected caustically, irritated by the evidence that Alex had wasted so little time before finding female companionship.

'Mrs Gantry, are you listening to me?'

Francis' frustrated voice came to her ears as if from a distance, and with a feeling of contrition, Olivia forced herself to concentrate. 'I'm sorry, Francis,' she said, smoothing her fine suede gloves between her fingers. 'I'm afraid I didn't hear what you said. Would you mind repeating it?'

'I can't believe you mean to go through with this, Mrs Gantry.' Francis stared at her imploringly. 'Surely there's some other way. Give Alex Gantry the money you offered me; pay him off! Given time you won't lose by it.'

'And the Gantry corporation marches on regardless!'

'Is that so important?'

'Yes, it is.' Olivia got up from her chair and walked to the windows, a slim elegant figure in her mink coat and pearls. She had dressed with especial care to come to the office, knowing she would be subjected to the most intense scrutiny, from the minute she entered the lobby downstairs. 'I married Henry to get my revenge. Do you think I'm particular what form that revenge takes?'

Francis had risen also, and now he came round the desk to stand beside it. 'You don't mind that it's Alex

Gantry who is going to profit from it?' he probed. 'He is Henry's son, after all. Do you really want to hand it to him on a plate?'

Olivia caught her breath. 'Don't try to change my mind, Francis.'

'Why not?' His tone was ironic now. 'What have I got to lose?'

Olivia glanced sideways at him, suddenly aware of a certain tautness about his features, a grimness around his mouth. Not for the first time she thought how attractive his clean-cut features were, and in so doing realised there was more than bitterness in his face.

'Francis!' she exclaimed, his name barely audible on her lips, and he bowed his head a little ruefully as she identified his meaning. 'Oh, Francis—I don't know what to say.'

'Don't say anything,' he advised her softly. 'I'm surprised it didn't occur to you before. I haven't exactly been able to hide my feelings.'

'You underestimate yourself.' Olivia needed time to assimilate this new development. She had never dreamt that Francis might have more than her business interests at heart, and it was another complication.

'Why do you think I haven't betrayed what you told me to the other members of the board?' he asked, holding her startled gaze with his, and Olivia shook her head.

'I assumed—for the money.'

'The quarter of a million you spoke of?' Francis shook his head. 'I could get at least four times that amount for the information you gave me.'

Olivia blinked. 'So why haven't you?'

'Do you have to ask?'

Olivia tried to think. 'Francis—I don't think——'

'Please,' he interrupted her, 'don't say anything now. I know it's too soon—I realise you have other things on your mind. But I wanted you to know you weren't alone in this.'

'Oh, Francis!' Olivia's fingers touched his sleeve half tentatively. 'It's so good to know there's at least one person I can trust. I'm so—confused!'

He put his hand over her fingers, pressing them against his arm for a moment. Then, gently, he guided her back to the desk. 'Tell me about Gantry,' he said. 'Tell me what you know about him. I think before you give him any authority, we should find out what he's been doing for the past fifteen years.'

'Well——' Olivia hesitated, 'I know he's spent some time in Tsaba, but that's all really. He's involved in a mining company, with another man—his partner. Unfortunately, his partner's dead now. That's probably why he was coming back to England.'

'I understood Cosgrove had sent for him.'

'Oh, yes. I think Adam did inform him of his father's death. But, according to Alex, he was intending to return.'

'I see,' Francis nodded. 'And has he any plans? I mean, does he talk to you about what he intends to do?'

Olivia shook her head. 'I don't think he'd tell me anything,' she replied flatly. 'He doesn't even like me.'

Francis frowned. 'That wasn't exactly my impression.'

To her annoyance, Olivia felt the hot colour flooding her cheeks. 'You were meant to think that. Good heavens, Francis, you don't honestly believe I would have anything to do with Alex Gantry!'

'I hope not.'

Olivia gasped. 'I assure you, I have nothing but contempt for the way he behaved. Since then I've hardly set eyes on him. As you know, I've been—unwell. I had a cold and I've been confined to my room. I haven't spoken with him since that morning.'

Francis acknowledged this with a reassuring gesture. 'I believe you, Mrs Gantry.' He considered for a moment, and then went on: 'Now—there's a board meeting next Tuesday. You won't be expected to attend, but I suggest I go along as your representative, and try to get us some kind of breathing space over the appointment. What do you say?'

Olivia moistened her lips. 'Could you do that?'

'I can try. I can explain that it would be too much of a strain, coming so soon after H.R.'s death, that you've been ill, and that you're not really up to it yet. They're sure to be sympathetic. Why not? So far as they're concerned, it's only a formality anyway. They'll be sure to think that you'll listen to their advice when the time comes.'

Olivia nodded. 'That sounds good.'

'Right,' Francis smiled. 'And now, shall we have some coffee? Or will you let me take you to lunch?'

'Some coffee would be fine,' Olivia agreed quietly, and while Francis went to instruct his secretary, she checked the knot of hair on top of her head with a nervous hand, to ensure that it was still in place.

It was very quiet in the office. This floor was sited sufficiently far from the ground to ensure that only the faintest hum of traffic noise penetrated the double-glazed windows, and she could even hear the clock ticking on the cabinet nearby. It was a huge building, she mused, reflecting how many people relied on the Gantry corporation for their livelihood. She hoped that she would not be responsible for throwing any of these people out of work. That had never been her intention, even though many of her father's loyal employees had lost their jobs in the melting pot of Henry's ambition. All she had wanted was to remove this living memorial to that ambition, and if that was impossible, to give control to the one man Henry had used her to disinherit.

Francis came back, but he was not alone: Sean Barrett was with him, and with them was Alex Gantry.

Sean Barrett was a man in his late fifties, who had worked for the corporation, in one form or another, for the past forty years. He was a big man, broad and running to fat now, with a huge belly protruding over his waistband. Olivia hardly knew him, but she knew Henry had thought highly of him, and in the cavalier world of boardroom politics, he could usually be relied on to support his chairman.

'Olivia,' he greeted her now, taking her hand and subjecting it to an emphatic squeeze. 'May I say you're a sight for sore eyes on this dull morning! What a pleasure it is to see such beauty in these drab surroundings!'

Olivia was forced to smile, but her eyes had moved automatically to the man behind Sean Barrett. Alex Gantry looked assured and irritatingly sophisticated in a sleek fitting three-piece charcoal business suit, and as different from the uncouth barbarian who had first invaded the library as it was possible to be. His mocking face derided her disconcertment, and she looked at Francis helplessly, desperate for an explanation.

'Your—stepson——' Francis evidently had difficulty in voicing this acknowledgement '—has been renewing his acquaintance with some of his old friends at Gantry House,' he told her stiffly, as one of the girls from the typing pool followed them into the room with a tray of coffee.

'Yes, that's right.' Sean Barrett stepped back to put a casual arm across Alex's shoulders. 'We've all known Alex since he was a little nipper, always getting into one scrape or another. I must admit, he's improved with age. I hardly recognised him.'

'Fifteen years is a long time, Sean,' Alex remarked

drily, leaving the older man to approach Olivia's chair. Ignoring her withdrawn expression, he squatted down beside her, taking one of her slim hands from her lap and holding on to it deliberately. 'I'm pleased to see you're feeling so much better,' he murmured, his dark eyes alight with devilry at her indignation. 'I've been worried about you.'

I bet you have, thought Olivia angrily, dragging her hand from his grasp and wishing she had the nerve to tell him so out loud. But instead she made some polite rejoinder, and Alex rose lithely to his feet to prop his hips against the desk only inches away from her. He was so close that when she crossed her legs, the tip of her shoe brushed the taut cloth of his trousers, and she removed her leg immediately, pressing her knees tightly together, in an unconscious attitude of rejection. A fleeting trace of humour crossed Alex's face at this revealing gesture, and she realised aggravatedly that he found her reactions laughable.

Whether Francis had been aware of this silent exchange, she could not be sure. It had all taken place in the space of a few seconds, and although Alex's present position beside her chair was infuriating, surely Francis could see that she did not like it. Heavens, she thought impatiently, when reason reasserted itself, she was actually beginning to feel guilty, about something over which she had no control.

Happily, Sean Barrett saw nothing amiss in Alex's apparent concern for his stepmother. 'I must say you surprise me, coming into the office like this, Olivia,' he said. 'Alex has just been telling me, you've not been well since the funeral.'

Olivia did not look up into Alex's dark face before replying: 'It was just a chill Mr Barrett. A severe cold, nothing more. I expect I was a little run down. This has been quite a strain.'

'Of course, it must have been.' Sean was all solicitude. 'But I'm pleased that you're feeling so much better. Can we look forward to your company at the board meeting on Tuesday? I expect Francis has put you in the picture. There are one or two matters which need your approval.'

Olivia looked despairingly at Francis, praying for his intervention, but to her surprise it was Alex who took up her cause. 'Don't you think you're being a bit premature, Sean?' he suggested, much to her astonishment. 'Liv's scarcely had time to consider her position. I mean, in her place I'd insist on a report, detailing all the different aspects of the company's operations, and an extraordinary audit of the books.'

Sean's short laugh was hardly one of amusement. 'But that is absolutely unnecessary, Alex. I mean, why should Olivia want this information? Of what use would it be to her? It's obvious that she could never consider taking over Henry's position. He wouldn't have expected it. He wouldn't have wanted it. Wouldn't it be simpler if we left the economics of the corporation to someone who can understand them, who could periodically provide Olivia with an ongoing report, should she feel such a thing was in her best interests?'

'You're not afraid of opening the books, are you, Sean?' Alex enquired, in the same pleasant tone, and the older man snorted.

'Of course not. And you should know better than to ask such a thing.'

'I think I can provide Mrs Gantry with all the information she needs,' Francis interposed smoothly at this point. 'Don't you agree, Mrs Gantry? We have discussed this matter at some length.'

His eyes met Olivia's, delivering an unmistakable message, but for once Olivia chose to ignore his advice. She realised Alex had his own reasons for delaying her eventual meeting with the board, but the idea of a report was appealing. Such a report was bound to take some time to prepare, thus alleviating the necessity for her to lie about her health. Pretending to be ill could be so restricting, and this way she might even learn something.

'I think—I think Alex has a point,' she ventured, earning a frown from two quarters. 'I didn't take much interest in the business when Henry was alive, but I'm prepared to make the effort. Surely you don't object, Mr Barrett. I would appreciate your co-operation.'

Sean Barrett moved his heavy shoulders in a somewhat defeated gesture. 'Naturally, you have my co-operation in all things, Olivia,' he declared shortly. 'But such a report may take several weeks to collate.'

'That's all right.' Olivia breathed more freely. 'I've got plenty of time.'

'Very well.' The big man turned towards the door. 'Coming, Alex? As you appear to have achieved your objective in coming here, I think you owe me the price of a drink, don't you?'

'My pleasure,' remarked Alex lazily, pushing himself up from the desk. 'I'll see you later, Liv. I've got something I want to discuss with you.'

Olivia looked up politely, but she avoided his eyes, and only after the door had closed behind them did she permit herself to look at Francis.

'Well . . .' she said defiantly, as he spread his hands before her, 'at least it's given us a breathing spell.'

Francis shook his head. 'I don't trust Gantry. He's got something up his sleeve. I'd have preferred to deal with this matter our own way.'

'But, Francis——' Olivia sighed, 'what can Alex do to me, if I'm already prepared to appoint him as chairman?'

Francis sat down at his desk, pulling the neglected

coffee tray towards him and carefully pouring two cups. 'Who knows what Alex Gantry may do?' he exclaimed, pushing one of the cups and the cream and sugar towards her. 'You saw how Sean reacted when Alex made his proposition. How do you propose to sell him to the rest of the board when his own uncle practically disowned him?'

'His uncle?' Olivia stared at him. 'Sean Barrett is Alex's uncle?'

'Sean's sister was H.R.'s first wife,' Francis explained patiently. 'Didn't H.R. tell you?'

'No.' Olivia shook her head. 'We didn't discuss his family.'

'Well, it's true. Elise Barrett married Henry Gantry in 1949. Alex was born a year later.'

Olivia absorbed this information with some astonishment. In Sean's position, she doubted she would have been so courteous to his brother-in-law's second wife. But diplomacy in business never ceased to amaze her, and this was just another example of the power Henry had wielded.

'Anyway,' Francis continued, drinking his coffee in gulps, 'I'd think very carefully before making a decision about this. I mean, do you have any idea how long it could take?'

'Does it matter?' Olivia realised his antipathy towards Alex Gantry more than equalled hers, and she quickly tried to reassure him. 'Whatever happens, I shan't forget your kindness, Francis. And you won't suffer by it, I'll see to that.'

She left the offices some twenty minutes later, going down in one of the high-speed lifts with some of the girls from the typing pool. They were evidently on their way to the staff canteen for lunch, and she was astonished to hear Alex Gantry's name entering their whispered conversation. Obviously they didn't know who she was, which was hardly surprising considering she had only visited the offices twice during the six months of her marriage, and they were consequently less cautious than they might otherwise have been.

'Did you see him?' one of the girls asked in a low tone. She was a pretty brunette, Olivia observed out of the corner of her eye, and the two girls with her were blondes. 'Honestly, he's nothing like his father.'

'No one, but no one, would want to be like Mr Gantry!' giggled one of the blondes. 'I heard he'd only come back because his father was dead!'

'Sssh!'

There was a whispered warning, and for a few moments Olivia could not hear what they were saying. But presently a word here and there came to her ears, and she detected the unmistakable drift of their speculations.

'I mean . . . younger than he is . . . how would you feel? . . . what do you think?'

Olivia's face was burning when she emerged from the lifts, and she was relieved the girls were going down to the basement restaurant when the commissionaire opened the door for her, and wished her good day. It would have been too humiliating to have them realise she might have overheard their chatter, and it was chastening, too, to imagine the depths to which such gossip could sink.

'Taxi, lady?'

The attractive male tones were unmistakable, and Olivia emerged from her reverie to find Alex blocking her path, a lazy smile adding to his disturbing attraction.

'No, thank you,' she refused at once, looking purposefully for the Rolls with Forsyth at the wheel. Francis would have telephoned the garage the minute she left his office, and by the time she got down to the ground floor her car should have been waiting.

'Well, that's a shame,' Alex remarked now, falling into step beside her as she crossed the paved forecourt of the building, and descended the steps to the street. 'I told Forsyth he wouldn't be needed and that I'd be driving you home.'

'You did *what*!' Olivia stopped then, and looked at him, but Alex was unrepentant beneath her indignant gaze.

'I sent Forsyth home,' he explained again, pushing his hands into the pockets of the leather coat he was wearing over his suit—a new one, obviously, thought Olivia in passing, since Henry had never possessed such an article—and permitting a rueful grimace. 'I thought we might have lunch together, before I show you the car I bought.'

'You must be out of your mind!' Olivia was incensed and frustrated, thinking of Forsyth driving home alone, believing she would welcome a lift from her stepson! 'Alex, I don't think this is very funny. It's too cold to play games of this sort.'

'I agree. And it's no game.' His eyes probed hers. 'So, have lunch with me, and I promise I'll drive you home straight after. Can't we at least pretend we have something in common?'

'I have nothing in common with you!' retorted Olivia hotly.

'Don't you?' Alex's eyes dropped insinuatingly to her mouth. 'Come on, Liv, don't fight me. You may not like the weapons I use in retaliation.'

Olivia's breathing had quickened in spite of herself. 'You wouldn't——'

'Wouldn't what? Kiss you, in full view of Barnes, our talkative commissionaire, and half a dozen gawping office girls? Don't tempt me, Liv. You might enjoy it.'

Olivia drew an unsteady breath. 'I hate you, Alex Gantry!'

'Well, that's a healthy emotion, at least. Now, let's take a cab to Mariani's, and you can tell me why you looked so red in the face when you came out of the building.'

Olivia stared at him in helpless confusion, but his words had alerted her to the fact that their conversation was no doubt being observed, and a swift glance over her shoulder confirmed this assumption.

'Call a cab,' she said, clenching her teeth, and with an infuriating smile he lifted his hand.

Immediately a cab pulled along beside them, and judging by its pace, Olivia guessed Alex had had it waiting all along. With a courteous gesture he opened the door for her, and she climbed into the back, shifting as far along the seat as it was possible to go. Alex gave his instructions to the driver before joining her, but when he did stretch his length beside her, he made no attempt to fill the space between them. On the contrary, he seemed quite content to view the traffic through half-closed eyes, the brooding lines around his mouth indicative of his meditation.

Mariani's was a restaurant in Piccadilly. Although Olivia had passed it on numerous occasions, she had never ventured within its distinguished portals. It was not a restaurant Henry had favoured; her husband had preferred the more recognised elegance of the Ritz only a few yards away. And she was surprised that Alex knew of such a place, which had not been open for more than seven or eight years.

But it appeared he was not unfamiliar with the staff there, and while Olivia was checking her coat in the silver and gilt surroundings of the cloakroom, Alex arranged for them to be shown to a corner table.

'Comfortable, isn't it?' he remarked, as he took his

seat on the banquette beside her. 'Mariani is an old friend. I generally try to come here at least once when I'm in London.'

Olivia stared at him with frosty eyes. 'I thought you said you'd lived in Tsaba for the past eight years. This place hasn't been open that long.'

'I wasn't a prisoner,' Alex replied mildly. 'And I don't recall denying coming back to England from time to time.'

Olivia gasped. 'And you never visited your father!'

Alex sighed. 'Look—let's leave that side of it, shall we? I didn't bring you here to start an argument over my relationship with your husband. I wanted to talk to you. Away from the cloying atmosphere of his house. Now, let me buy you a drink. What do you like? Martini, sherry, what?'

Olivia hesitated, but then realising it would be foolish to sit there without a drink, she acquiesced. 'I'll have a Martini,' she conceded shortly. 'With ice and soda.'

While Alex was ordering their drinks, Olivia took the opportunity to glance about her. Although the room was not large, it was well patronised, and she wondered apprehensively whether their identity had been observed. The restaurant itself was discreetly lit and intimate, the kind of place one might use for an indiscreet assignation. And that was what this was, she thought tensely, as she met Alex's disturbing dark gaze.

'So,' he said, when her Martini had been served and a squat tumbler, half filled with an amber-coloured liquid, had been set before him. 'You're looking a little less harassed now. What did Kennedy say to you after I left? I guess he wasn't too suited when you decided to back me.'

'I did not back you!' Olivia retorted, turning her glass between her palms. 'I—I merely agreed that a report would give us all a—a breathing space.'

Alex inclined his head. 'But Kennedy didn't agree.'

'He—he neither agreed nor disagreed.'

'He does what you tell him, right?'

Olivia flushed at the deliberate irony. 'Francis—Francis is a friend.'

'I'll bet he is!'

'You don't understand——'

'Nor do you.'

Olivia looked away from that mocking face. It was impossible to hold a discussion with him. He did not trust her, and after the things Francis had said, she had even less reason to trust him. It was an impossible situation, made the more so by her unwilling awareness of him as a man . . .

'At least tell me what he said to make you look so distraught,' Alex urged, and her eyes darted to his in swift confusion.

'He—Francis, that is—he didn't say anything.'

'Well, someone must have said something to upset you,' Alex persisted. 'And if it wasn't Kennedy, I wonder who——'

'It was nobody!' Olivia spoke vehemently. 'No one said anything to me, I tell you. I—I expect the cold air——'

'Ah, now I begin to understand.' Alex toyed with his glass, his mouth twisting wryly as he viewed her distress. 'It wasn't something that was said, it was something you overheard. From whom, I wonder? And where? In the lift?'

His perception was unnerving, but Olivia refused to satisfy him, and with a shrug he added: 'I guess it was to do with you and me. My presence in the building did cause quite a stir, and I can imagine how our relationship might be misconstrued.'

'You flatter yourself!' Olivia spoke in a low, angry tone. 'I doubt your arrival caused more than a flutter on the office grapevine.'

Alex lifted one shoulder in a curiously appealing gesture, and Olivia looked down into her glass as the familiar feeling of attraction prickled across her skin.

The arrival of the waiter with the menus was a welcome distraction, and while Alex discussed the relative merits of various dishes with the man, Olivia struggled to control her unruly emotions. It should not be so hard, she told herself desperately. This man was Henry's son, after all, and she had had no love for his father. And yet, without the complicating barrier of their relationship, she knew his identity would not have been enough . . .

'Does avocado appeal to you?' Alex was asking her now, and it was incredibly difficult to concentrate on food when her senses were arousing entirely different appetites.

'What? Avocado?' Olivia moistened her dry lips. 'Oh—oh, yes. That sounds very nice——'

'—and steak?' he prompted, and she nodded jerkily.

'Medium,' she agreed, wishing he would stop looking at her.

'You got that?' Alex asked, turning back to the waiter, and Olivia took a mouthful of her Martini in an effort to restore her equilibrium.

'Okay.' The waiter had departed, and Alex turned back to her. 'What's the matter? Did I miss something?'

Olivia shook her head. 'This—this Martini: it's rather sharp——'

Alex looked sceptical, but he didn't pursue it, much to her relief. Instead, he rested both his elbows on the table, and looking sideways at her he said: 'Why have you been avoiding me?'

'I haven't.'

Olivia responded instantly, but Alex was not going to let this topic go. 'What would you call it?'

'I've been ill.'

'You've had a cold. Mrs Winters told me.'

Olivia shrugged. 'Then you'll know the doctor confined me to my room.'

'So conveniently!'

Olivia trod more confidently: 'I was ill. I—I suppose it was the aftermath of your father's death. It has been a strain——'

'For someone who hated him?'

She ought to have expected it, she knew. Alex Gantry was not the kind of man to whom one could make a statement of that kind without there coming a time when she would have to explain herself. But she had been ready for it a week ago. Now she wasn't.

'Anyone's death is a strain,' she said evasively.

' "Any man's death diminishes me"—is that it?' he remarked drily. 'Do you read John Donne? If so, you'll know how that ends.'

Olivia forced herself to meet his gaze. 'Is that a threat?'

Alex shook his head. 'I just want to know what he did to make you hate him.'

Olivia drew a deep breath. 'I don't think that's any concern of yours.'

'On the contrary, I'm his son, and I have the right to wonder what happened to make you change towards him.'

'I didn't——' Olivia broke off abruptly, aware that she had almost betrayed herself. 'I didn't—change—towards him. Your—your father didn't—know.'

'That you hated him?' Alex pushed back the thick strands of ash-fair hair that had strayed across his forehead with a bewildered hand. 'Forgive me, I'm just a simple fellow; but I don't know what the hell you're talking about.'

'You don't have to,' replied Olivia composedly. 'Oh—

look! I think this is our mousse.'

The next few minutes were taken up with the waiter serving the mousse, and the wine waiter serving a bottle of red wine. It was a delicious claret, not too dry, and chambré to perfection, and Olivia took the opportunity to comment on the wine to avoid any further embarrassment. But Alex was not so easily diverted, and when the waiters had departed and they were alone again, he resumed his questioning:

'What happened?' he persisted, moving along the banquette so that his thigh was brushing hers. And when she looked up at him with wide startled eyes, he added: 'Didn't you want to go through with it? Did you really believe the old man wouldn't demand his pound of flesh!'

Olivia's lips parted. 'I don't know what you——'

'No wonder you find Kennedy so attractive. I guess he's been the only compensation you've had.'

Olivia gasped. 'You—you're despicable!'

'Why? Because I speak the truth. Because the picture of you going to bed with a man almost old enough to be your grandfather makes me sick to my stomach! You must have been pretty desperate, that's all I can say.'

'You—*bastard*!'

Alex's eyes glittered. 'Don't tempt me, Liv. Right now, I'm choked enough to make you pay for those words!'

Olivia forced back a sob. 'Why? Because they're true?' she taunted, and Alex impaled her with a look.

'I warned you,' he said, his dark gaze shifting to her mouth. 'Like father, like son, isn't that what they say?'

'Don't be so ridiculous——'

'Let's find out, shall we?' he grated, and his hand at her nape brought her mouth to his.

His lips were flavoured with wine, warm and soft and sensual, and in no way the assault they had been previously. For a heart-stopping moment, she was too shocked to resist him, and she could feel his lips against hers, coaxing them apart, seeking the moist sweetness within. Then horror at what she was doing brought her back from the brink.

'No——' she choked against his lips, trying to drag herself away, but although his mouth was gentle, his hold on her was not. His free hand was gripping her thigh with a painful intensity, imprisoning her to the seat, and imprisoning her in his grasp. Things her mother had told her, ways of defending herself in these circumstances, flooded her confused brain, but only her hands were free, and the idea of delivering a blow where it would hurt him filled her with revulsion. She couldn't do it; she could only steel herself against him, and pray that the seclusion of their table and the discreet lighting in the restaurant would conceal what was happening.

When he finally set her free, he was breathing hard, and his lean face was paler beneath his tan. Instead of eating his mousse, he pushed the plate aside, and finishing the wine in his glass, he poured himself some more with hands that were not quite steady.

'Point proved, I think,' he said at last, his voice harsh and accusing. 'My God, Liv, do you really expect me to believe a man of nearly seventy could satisfy you? You were cheating him all along the line. Admit it!'

Olivia had taken the few minutes when he had been pouring his wine to compose herself, and now she found she could answer him quite calmly, even though her nerves were as taut as violin strings. 'I don't intend to admit anything to you, Mr Gantry! You can believe what you like. What you can't do is make me hate myself any more than I do already. Now, shall we abandon this abortive attempt at conviviality, and go our separate ways?'

'No!' To her astonishment, Alex's fingers about her

wrist prevented her from rising. 'No, *Mrs* Gantry, I haven't finished with you yet. Like I told you the other day, my father may have married you, but I'm here to see you don't enjoy being his widow!'

CHAPTER SIX

OLIVIA was beginning to believe she must be quite mad to consider putting Alex Gantry in a position of command. Francis was right. He was untrustworthy, and completely unscrupulous; and although she found excuses for his bitterness in the arbitrary terms of his father's will, she could not excuse his behaviour towards her.

He had no respect for her, that was obvious, and he evidently believed she had been as unscrupulous as himself in persuading his father to marry her. She doubted he would believe the truth, even if she told it to him, and in any case, the idea of doing that was not one she seriously considered. There were limits to the sacrifice she was prepared to make, she discovered, and the longer she knew Alex Gantry, the more sympathy she had with his father.

It was a terrible situation. It should have been simple, but it wasn't, and as in all things, personalities coloured opinions. It was all very well deciding to give Alex back what was rightfully his when he was just a faceless name from the past. Knowing him in the flesh, learning what manner of man he was, and how easily he could overwhelm her inhibitions, was another thing altogether, and despite her good intentions, she was torn by the knowledge of the weaknesses he could exploit. Dear God, she thought fearfully, she knew what would happen if she continued to live in Henry's house: sooner or later, Alex would decide that she was as much his to control as the Gantry corporation, and that was something she could never allow. But how could she prevent it when her own body betrayed her, every time he touched her?

If only she was more experienced, she thought, re-membering those occasions when she had had dates in the past that had never progressed farther than a furtive fumbling in the dark of a parked car. Sex was not something she had ever been curious about. Instead, she had been amused when some young man attempted to arouse her with groping fingers, and her laughter had proved a very adequate form of protection. She had passed her university days without any desire for a seri-ous commitment, and when she had accepted Henry's offer of marriage she had done so in the belief that she was incapable of having a sexual relationship.

How wrong she had been, she flayed herself bitterly. From the minute she met Alex, from the minute she encountered those night-dark eyes, she had been fighting a losing battle against his attraction; and while she was not naïve enough to imagine that what she felt for him was love, she knew that when he touched her, she wanted to touch him, too.

With such thoughts for company, the journey back to Chalcott was not the most comfortable Olivia had spent. Seated with Alex, in the sleek grey Maserati he had acquired for his own use, she was intensely conscious of the lean length of him, relaxed beside her. He was so cool, she thought angrily, so sure of himself; while she was living on her nerves and despising the awareness she had of his lithe muscled body.

'Do you like the car?' he enquired at one point, caus-ing her to glance his way in reluctant acquiescence.

'Does it matter?' she demanded tautly, dragging her eyes from the long brown fingers stroking the wheel, and he inclined his head.

'It should,' he remarked carelessly. 'Considering you paid for it. You're very generous. I must remember that when our positions are reversed.'

Olivia's face mirrored her disbelief. '*I* paid for it?' she echoed.

'Of course.' Alex shifted more comfortably in his seat. 'You did tell me to get a car of my own, didn't you? The garage proprietor was most appreciative of your custom.'

Olivia expelled her breath noisily. 'You—you—how dare you? I did not offer to pay for a car for you! Naturally, I assumed——'

'And naturally I assumed you wouldn't want your stepson running around in an old banger,' retorted Alex mildly, not at all perturbed by her outraged face. 'Come on, Liv! It's a beautiful car. Admit it! How could I offer to drive you home in some old rattletrap?'

'I didn't need you to drive me home,' replied Olivia icily. 'Oh, you're completely unprincipled, aren't you? You're determined to cause as much trouble as you possibly can.'

'I did warn you,' he replied evenly. 'By the way, would you have any objections if I invited a guest to stay for a few days?'

Olivia stared at him. 'Yes,' she said angrily. 'Yes, I would object. Don't imagine you're going to use my home as some kind of dosshouse for every hanger-on you choose to befriend!'

'It's a female, actually,' Alex told her without emphasis, and Olivia's temper exploded.

'You dare to suggest bringing some girl-friend of yours into the house!' she spat furiously. 'My God, you've got a nerve! Not only do you come and force your way into my house, but you're actually suggesting I entertain your mistress——'

'She's not my mistress,' Alex interrupted her harshly, his own temper surfacing after that cutting accusation. 'She's just someone I know. A friend, if you like. Someone who'd like to meet you.'

'Well, I don't want to meet any friend of yours!' retorted Olivia, too incensed to think reasonably. 'In fact, I think it would be better if you found somewhere else to stay. You can always lease a flat in my name. Just as you got this car.'

'You really are a bitch, aren't you, Liv?' he said, his lips curling contemptuously. 'What's the matter? What are you afraid of suddenly? Isn't the house big enough for both of us? I don't intend our joint tenancy to last indefinitely, you know.'

Olivia turned her head away to stare out of the window, her anger evaporating to leave a horribly flat feeling. What was she doing? *What was she doing?* Couldn't she at least sustain a pretence at civility, even if it was only a veneer? As Alex had said, the situation could not last much longer, and once the report was produced . . .

'I'm sorry,' she got out at last, without looking at him, noticing with relief that they were already passing through the outskirts of Chalcott. They would be home in less than ten minutes. Virginia Drive was situated on the far side of the small country town, only a couple of miles from its centre. 'I—it's foolish for us to go on like this. Can't we at least attempt to be civil with one another?'

'On whose terms?' Alex asked tersely, and she glanced round at him.

'I don't know what you mean.'

'I mean—exactly what are you suggesting? That we go on as before?'

'I—I suppose so.'

'And—Lilian?'

Olivia's cheek muscles stiffened. 'Lilian?' she echoed. 'You mean—this girl-friend of yours?'

'Who else?' Alex took his eyes from the road for a moment to meet her indignant gaze. 'Do I get your permission to invite her to stay?'

Olivia sighed. 'Alex——'

'Well?'

She bent her head and pulled off her gloves with jerky movements. The idea of allowing some strange female into the house was not attractive, but it might mean her salvation. Surely, with some other girl to distract his attention, she might view their relationship more objectively.

'Who is she?' she asked now, without looking at him. 'You called her Lilian. I—I gather she isn't the—the girl who—who's been telephoning you.'

Alex made a derisive sound. 'Who told you about that? Oh, don't bother to answer, I can guess. Mrs Winters. And yes, as it happens, it is the same girl.'

Olivia's brows were drawn as she gazed at him. 'But her name was Missy. And—and it wasn't Mrs Winters who told me. It was Mary.'

'Missy!' Alex caught an amused breath. 'You mean— *Miss Eve*! Lilian Eve. Get it?'

'Oh!' Olivia pressed her gloves between her cold fingers. 'I see.'

'And?'

Olivia shook her head. 'Invite her if you must,' she exclaimed tautly, and thereafter maintained an uneasy silence until the gates of the house were reached.

She had dinner with Alex that evening. They ate in the dining room, the long polished table lit with scented candles, whose golden flames cast an edge of gilt over silver knives and forks and fine fluted glass. Outside, the darkness of the verandah and the terraced gardens beyond cast back their reflections through the glass, the candles moving in the draught causing the image to shimmer like summer heat.

Olivia had dressed with care, the demureness of her

high-necked blouse and ankle-length skirt a deliberate
attempt to maintain the distance of their relationship.

But she need not have bothered. Alex was morose,
remote; eating what was put before him without really
noticing it, and offering no more in the way of conversation than the perfunctory exchanges necessary to the
task. He was evidently involved with some inner conflict,
and Olivia had plenty of time to admire the elegant cut
of his dark green velvet dinner jacket, which contrasted
so attractively with his light hair and tanned skin. She
didn't want to look at him; she didn't want to find anything attractive in his indolent appearance; but the fact
remained that her eyes did linger on the bleached hair
that brushed his collar at the back of his neck, and on
the brown skin of his wrists emerging from his cuffs.

When the meal was over he excused himself abruptly,
and when Mrs Winters served her coffee in the library
she did so with the information that Master Alex had
taken himself off.

'I thought he might have stayed in this evening, seeing
as how it's your first evening downstairs, Mrs Gantry,'
she declared, in mild admonition, and then qualified this
statement by saying that he had said something about
seeing Mr Cosgrove, and that she supposed his father's
solicitor would be glad to see him.

Olivia absorbed this information sceptically. She
doubted Alex had taken himself off so eagerly just to
see Adam Cosgrove. But she didn't argue with Mrs
Winters, and when the housekeeper had left her, she
determinedly found herself a book and tried to read.

The following day she was left very much to her own
devices. Alex disappeared after breakfast, and although
Olivia told herself she was glad when the Maserati
roared off down the drive, human nature being what it
is, she was intently curious as to his destination. Had he
gone to see the mysterious Miss Eve? Or had he

arranged to meet Adam Cosgrove again? She had no way of knowing, and when bedtime came, and he still had not returned, curiosity gave way to resentment.

The telephone rang next morning while she was having a solitary breakfast, and answering it, she heard Adam Cosgrove's voice.

'Mrs Gantry?' He sounded relieved. 'Oh, Olivia, I hope I'm not calling at an inconvenient time.'

'Not at all.' Olivia was curious. She couldn't imagine why Adam Cosgrove might be calling her. Unless it had something to do with Alex! 'Er—is something wrong?'

'No, nothing. Nothing at all. I—just wondered if we could arrange a meeting, Olivia. There are one or two things we have to discuss.'

'Of course.' In the upheaval of Alex's arrival and her subsequent illness, Olivia had forgotten her promise to the older man. 'Whenever you say. This afternoon, if you like.'

'That would be fine.' Adam sounded pleased. 'I'll look forward to it.'

'Yes. Yes, so will I.' Olivia made her farewells, but she returned the receiver to its rest with a troubled frown. Somehow she had the feeling that Adam's call was more than just an invitation to discuss the administration of Henry's will, and she couldn't help associating it with Mrs Winters' information of two nights ago. Had Alex really gone to see Adam Cosgrove, and if so, why? Was it just because they were old friends, or had he had more personal matters on his mind? Somehow, the idea of Alex confiding in Adam Cosgrove without her knowledge filled her with an unreasoning resentment that she did not try to analyse. So these were the *terms* he had spoken of! How much more was she expected to take?

Deciding she would prefer to avoid Alex until after this interview, Olivia left the study and went up to her room to change. She had decided she would have lunch in Chalcott, and after arranging with Forsyth to have the car at the door in fifteen minutes, she took off the skirt and sweater she had been wearing, and replaced them with a purple suede trouser suit. A fur jacket completed the ensemble, and she was about to leave the room to go downstairs, when Mary knocked at the door.

'You're going out?' she exclaimed, pausing to view Olivia's appearance with approving eyes. 'Master Alex asked me to find you. He wants to speak to you.'

'Then he'll have to wait, won't he?' replied Olivia tautly, picking up her handbag. 'Forsyth is waiting for me, Mary. I—er—I have an appointment in Chalcott. Tell Mr Gantry I'll speak to him when I get back.'

'And when will you be back, Mrs Gantry?' Mary asked bewilderedly. 'I mean—couldn't you just spare a minute——'

'No, I couldn't.' Olivia was waiting for the other girl to move out of the doorway, and when Mary unwillingly did so, she passed her with a tight smile. 'Tell Mrs Winters I won't be in to lunch, will you?' she added crisply, and walked away along the corridor before any further protest was forthcoming.

It was a chilly March day, but Chalcott was busy with people shopping for the weekend ahead, and Olivia welcomed the comforting anonymity of crowds of people. Telling Forsyth she would ring when she wanted him to come back for her, she dismissed the chauffeur, and spent the rest of the morning wandering round the shopping precinct. Occasionally she was recognised, she knew that, from the furtive glances she received from shop assistants, who whispered to their colleagues behind hastily erected barriers. It was an experience she had been forced to get used to since her marriage to Henry Gantry, her youth and beauty providing more than enough interest for the avid gossip columnists. However, since Henry's last illness, she had spent little time in public places, and it was rather unnerving to find his death had not changed her image as his widow.

The idea of lunching in some public restaurant therefore became less appealing. Wherever she went, someone was bound to recognise her, and rather than find herself the cynosure of so many curious eyes, she bought herself a sandwich and a can of coke, and took them to the park.

Fortunately the weather meant that few people ventured into the park on such an afternoon. There was only one other adult there, a girl of perhaps her own age or a little older, accompanied by a toddler wearing a fleecy red jump-suit. They were playing a game with a ball, and Olivia idly watched their antics, enjoying the sense of freedom they evoked. The baby, for he was little more, was quite adorable, and noticing how brown his skin was, Olivia was reminded of Alex. Like Alex, the baby had evidently spent some time in a warmer climate. No one could look so rudely healthy after a damp winter in England, and she guessed the girl's husband must be employed overseas.

The girl herself was slim and attractive, with burnished brown hair and an alert pointed face. She was not at all tanned, but her skin was of that pale, magnolia fairness that seldom gains any colour, and Olivia had little doubt that she was the baby's mother. She found herself envying the girl's happiness, the simple pleasure she obviously gained from playing with her little son— or daughter, Olivia was not sure which—and the irony of her own position struck her with a painful intensity. That she should find herself attracted to a man who not only despised her and everything she stood for, but who was forbidden to her by the very vows she had taken so unwillingly. She and her mother were the same: they were both destined to suffer at the hands of the Gantrys.

Adam Cosgrove was awaiting her when she arrived at his office a little after two o'clock. His secretary greeted her sympathetically, offering her own condolences over Henry's death, and then showed her into Adam's office with the deference afforded to her position.

'Olivia!' Adam took her hand warmly before ushering her into the chair opposite his. 'You're looking much better. I was sorry to hear you'd been taken ill so soon after the funeral.'

Olivia subsided into the seat and managed a faint smile. 'Just a cold, Mr Cosgrove,' she assured him evenly. 'I'm sorry, too. I should have rung you sooner. I forgot all about our previous arrangement.'

'That's all right.' Adam seated himself behind his desk and viewed her understandingly. 'I expect you've had other things on your mind.'

Olivia bit her lip. 'You know that Alex is back.'

Adam's hesitation was barely perceptible. 'Yes. Yes, I know.'

'Of course, he came to see you, didn't he?' Olivia was not finding this easy, and nor, she hazarded, was he. 'You wrote to him. You should have told me.'

Adam's lips twisted. 'Yes. Yes, perhaps I should. But, as Henry knew where he was and made no effort to get in touch with him . . .'

'Henry knew!' Olivia's dark brows arched.

'I did inform him of Alex's whereabouts, from time to time.'

'I see.' Olivia realised she had leant forward in her chair and deliberately forced herself to relax again. 'Henry didn't mention that to me.'

'He wouldn't,' Adam shrugged. 'But it's all water under the bridge now——'

'What is?' Olivia met his wry gaze. 'Mr Cosgrove,

isn't it about time I was told why Henry chose to cut Alex out of his will?'

Adam frowned. 'If he didn't tell you——'

'But as Henry's dead now, the information can't hurt him, can it? And—and it might help me.'

'Help you?' Adam looked curious. 'How?'

Olivia sighed. 'To get to know Alex better. He—well, as you can imagine, he and I are not exactly on the best of terms at present, and it's very difficult to put your point of view if you don't understand the situation.'

Adam studied her animated features for a few moments, then got heavily up from his chair. 'Olivia, I'm not sure—I'm not sure getting to know—this young man will serve any useful purpose.'

'What do you mean?' Olivia looked up at him. 'Surely it would serve a very useful purpose?'

'Olivia, you mustn't let anyone force you into doing something you might later regret!'

'Regret?' Olivia was confused. 'How—regret?'

Adam sighed now, pacing across the room with slow deliberation. 'I realise you might feel—obligated,' he said, after some consideration, 'but really, it's not something you should rush into.'

Olivia looked down at her hands, trying to make some sense of what he was trying to say. She had come here, prepared to defend her rights as Henry's heir, and instead Adam seemed to be trying to warn her. But warn her about what?

'I thought—I assumed you were Alex's friend,' she ventured at last, and Adam made a sound of impatience before resuming his seat.

'I am,' he said. 'I—am Alex's friend. But I'm your friend, Olivia, and I was H.R.'s friend, too.'

Olivia licked her lips. 'You're saying you don't trust Alex, is that it?'

Adam expelled his breath wearily. 'I'm saying that

perhaps there are circumstances here that you should consider very seriously before doing anything.'

Olivia was completely mystified, and she looked it. 'Mr Cosgrove, has Francis Kennedy spoken to you?'

'Francis?' Adam looked puzzled. 'No. At least, not since the evening after the funeral. We had dinner together.'

'Yes. Yes, he told me. But you didn't mention to him that Alex was back.'

'I saw no reason to do so. Not at that time.'

'No,' Olivia nodded. 'So Francis hasn't said anything to you about—about the corporation?'

'No.' Adam shook his head. 'But I understand that you have asked for a full report before you announce any new appointments.'

Alex! thought Olivia caustically. So he had been here two nights ago.

'That's right,' she said now, toying with the strap of her handbag. 'I think that's fair, don't you?'

'It was my intention to advise you to tread carefully before making any commitment,' Adam agreed. 'And it gives you time to consider all options.'

'Yes.' Olivia's smile was tight, but Adam didn't seem to notice. 'Tell me,' she went on, 'what would you do, in my position? About Alex, I mean.'

This was evidently a question he was not prepared for, and the nervous way his fingers fiddled with the inkstand on the desk revealed his agitation. 'I?' he said, to gain some time. 'My dear Olivia, I think you know H.R.'s wishes as well as I do. Perhaps my best advice to you is to remember that you were his wife, and he left the corporation in your hands.'

Olivia uttered an aggravated sound. 'You said yourself you'd tried to change Henry's mind!'

'Without success.'

'But Alex is here?'

'He chose to walk out on his father,' Adam replied quietly. 'And the way things have turned out, he hasn't exactly covered himself with glory, has he?'

'Why not? Why did he walk out on his father? Mr Cosgrove, you must tell me. He—he's my stepson. How can I be objective about something I don't know?'

Adam rested his elbows on the arms of his chair and steepled his fingers. 'What do you really know about Alex? What did H.R. tell you?'

'Nothing. Absolutely nothing.'

'Hmm.' Adam was thoughtful. 'And what about his first wife? Alex's mother. Did H.R. tell you how she died?'

'No.' Olivia frowned. 'I assumed she had some illness . . .'

'She was drowned.' Adam's lips jutted. 'Elise was drowned. She was found in the river, not far from the house.'

'Oh, how awful!' Olivia was appalled. 'Was there an accident?' She was remembering what Alex had said about a boat sinking. 'Poor Henry!'

'Yes.' Adam sounded less sympathetic. 'It was terrible. But it was no accident, I'm afraid.'

Olivia stared at him. 'You mean—she was murdered!'

'Nothing so dramatic, my dear. She committed suicide. She couldn't swim, you see, so she took Alex's dinghy out into midstream and sank it.'

Olivia shook her head. 'But—but why?'

'It's a long story . . .'

'I'd still like to hear it.'

Adam bent his head to rest his chin on the tips of his fingers. 'You may not like what you hear.'

'I'm prepared to risk it.'

'Very well.' Adam drew a deep breath. 'She killed herself because she found out H.R. was having an affair with another woman.'

Olivia stiffened. 'Another woman?'

'That's right.' Adam's nostrils flared. 'I told you you might not like it.'

'It doesn't matter.' Olivia was impatient. 'Please—go on.'

'Well, let me see, it must be all of twenty years ago now, maybe longer. H.R. was in the process of building his empire.' His tone was wry. 'Some woman—the wife of a man he was doing business with—attracted his attention. I don't know all the details. I only know Elise found out and when H.R. refused to give up this woman, she took her own life.'

Olivia was trembling now. The connotations were too precise. There had to be a connection between what Adam was relating and what her mother had told her.

'Anyway, it was all hushed up,' Adam said tersely. 'Alex was only a child, not much more than eight years old, I suppose, and H.R. didn't want a scandal. Unfortunately, as it turned out, H.R. was not the only one to suffer from that tragic affair.'

'You mean—Alex?'

'The boy blamed himself, you see.' Adam spoke flatly. 'It was his dinghy. He didn't understand what had happened, of course, and in his eyes his mother's death was due to him.'

'Olivia's fingers were curled into tight balls. 'But surely—Henry explained——'

'I'm afraid not.' Adam's hands fell heavily to the arms of his chair. 'It was easier, you see, to let the boy believe——'

'—that he was his mother's murderer!'

'Not that.' Adam was evidently trying to be objective. 'Olivia, H.R. thought it would be healthier for the boy not to learn why his mother died. At least, not then.'

Olivia felt sick. She could imagine how Alex must have felt, lost and alone, deprived of the mother he had known and loved. He must have blamed himself utterly for everything that had happened, and how that guilt would weigh on a boy of eight!

'I—I suppose—he found out,' she ventured, and Adam nodded.

'Eventually. Someone must have told him—H.R. never found out who. I think he suspected Sean Barrett, but he could never prove anything, and besides, what could he say? It was the truth.' He sighed. 'Alex never forgave his father.'

Olivia tried to absorb this new information. It certainly explained Alex's feelings towards his father. To allow a boy to shoulder a burden that should not have been his in the first place was an intolerable crime, and it made Henry's reasons for cutting his son out of his will even less acceptable. Olivia shook her head. She had thought she had reasons for hating Henry Gantry, but compared to Alex's experience, her own seemed insignificant. After all, without her mother's involvement Alex's mother might still be alive. It would be asking too much of coincidence to believe that some other woman had been around at the same time, and it was irony indeed that that woman's daughter should now stand between him and his inheritance. Or had that been Henry's plan? Had marrying her been the final denunciation? She doubted she would ever know, but at least her own course of action seemed clear to her now.

'Mr Cosgrove.' She moistened her lips with a nervous tongue before continuing: 'Mr Cosgrove, do you remember, just after the funeral, when we discussed Henry's will?'

'Of course.' Adam inclined his head.

'And do you remember I expressed some disappointment at the terms of the will?'

'I think you were distraught, Olivia. It's difficult for someone without the experience to understand how an organisation like the Gantry corporation works.'

'Yes.' Olivia was prepared to let that go. 'Well, I—I've had some time to think about this, and—and after considering all the facts, I think I'd like to propose Alex as chairman.'

'You can't.'

Adam's denial was firm and compelling, and Olivia stared at him blankly, bewildered by his reaction. She had expected he, of all of them, would approve her recommendation, and his brusque negation was both disappointing and baffling.

'I can't?' she echoed now. 'Why? Surely, after what you've just told me, Alex Gantry has as much right as anyone to take his father's place. Oh, he may not have the experience, I've no doubt he will need some assistance to begin with, but as he's Henry's son his claim should be indisputable!'

Adam lay back in his chair, regarding her with troubled grey eyes. 'Olivia, have you ever considered Alex might not be who he says he is? Do you really know that he's H.R.'s son? Do you have any definite proof?'

Olivia's lips parted. 'Proof? *Proof?* But you know he is. I mean, everyone recognises him.'

'It's fifteen years since anyone has set eyes on Alex Gantry,' retorted Adam flatly. 'Oh, the likeness is there, I'm not denying that. But is it enough? Olivia, I can understand how you feel, and your motives are laudable, but until I know a little more about the man who says he is your stepson, I don't think we should rush our fences!'

CHAPTER SEVEN

ALEX was not at home when Olivia got back to the house, and she thought that was just as well. She needed time to assimilate what Adam Cosgrove had told her, and with Alex around, coherent thought was impossible.

. Until that afternoon, she realised, she had never doubted Alex's identity. Mrs Winters had accepted him, and she had done the same, quite simply because there had seemed no room for flaws. But if he was not who he said he was, he was obviously someone who had known Alex very well, and it was a little unnerving to contemplate the possibility of having a stranger in the house.

The reasons why anyone should impersonate Alex Gantry were less difficult to probe. He was Henry Gantry's son, after all, and as such might be expected to be worth a small fortune. Alex Gantry himself had not known the terms of his father's will, and money, as always, was an irresistible magnet.

Shedding her jacket in her room, Olivia shook her head at Adam's calm acceptance of the situation. Somehow she would have expected him to be more concerned for her, but perhaps his sympathies had been strained by her own protests over the will. Perhaps he, like Francis, had suspicions about her, about her relationship with the man they all knew as Alex Gantry. Had she, by announcing her intentions, innocently aroused those suspicions, or was Adam simply stalling her from making her intentions public?

Her head ached with the complexity of it all. Adam's

assurances that he was having Alex's claims investigated had not rung completely true. Surely, if he had any suspicions that Alex was an impostor, he should voice them openly. How could he allow her to go on living in the same house as a man who could be a confidence trickster, a swindler, or worse! If he was not Alex, where was Alex Gantry? Perhaps that was something she should find out for herself.

She did not see Alex that day. He had not returned at dinner time, and Olivia had a light meal served in her room preferring to avoid any involuntary encounter with the man she knew as her stepson. She spent the evening in a state of some tension, torn by the knowledge that half of her wished that Alex was not who he said he was. If he was not her stepson, the attraction she felt towards him was not something of which she need feel ashamed. But if he was not her stepson, a small voice argued, what manner of man was he? It was a no-win position, and she went to bed without coming to any satisfactory conclusion.

She did not sleep well, and she was still awake when the distinctive sound of the Maserati's engine purred up the drive. The sound was extinguished in the cavernous surroundings of the garage, and then later, she heard Alex ascending the stairs. Her shoulders hunched instinctively at the awareness of him only feet away along the corridor. She was not alarmed exactly, but after what Adam had intimated, she was acutely sensitive, and it was hours before her brain would allow her to relax.

The following morning she was seated at the table in the dining room, drinking her second cup of coffee while she opened the mail, when Alex appeared in the doorway.

'Preparing for another swift getaway?' he enquired drily, advancing into the room, and Olivia felt her cheeks darken with colour.

'No,' she said shortly. 'Why should I?'

'You tell me,' remarked Alex, lifting the coffee pot that was set in front of her and calculating its weight. 'You apparently hadn't a minute to spare yesterday,' he added, helping himself to a cup of the hot aromatic liquid.

'I—I had an appointment,' Olivia declared, realising as she did so she was speaking defensively. Steeling herself against the almost irresistible impulse to tell him what Adam Cosgrove had said, she lifted her shoulders. 'I didn't know I had to check my movements with you.'

Alex's mouth drew into a downward slant. 'That was uncalled for. I just wanted to speak to you, that's all.'

'What about?'

The question was out before she could prevent it, but Alex didn't seem at all perturbed. 'It was about Lilian, actually,' he replied, and she realised she had forgotten all about his girl-friend's intended arrival.

'Oh——' She put down her cup with careful deliberation. 'I—did you speak to Mrs Winters?'

'I think that's your prerogative, not mine,' he retorted flatly. 'As a matter of fact, it's probably just as well you haven't—yet.'

'You mean—she's not coming?' Olivia could hardly keep the relief out of her voice, but Alex quickly discouraged her.

'On the contrary. With your permission, of course,' this was said with irony, 'she'll be here this afternoon. But there is a complication.'

Olivia fingered the slender gold chain that circled her throat. 'A complication?'

'Yes.' Alex picked up a chair, swung it round and straddled it, facing her with his arm across the back.

'She's not alone. She wants to bring her son with her.'

'Her son?' Olivia was astounded. 'She's married?'

'Did I say so?' Alex spoke indolently. 'Or in your small world can there be no other explanation?'

'You said her son——'

'So I did. But Lilian is not married. Surely someone of your—shall we say—experience should understand her difficulties.'

Olivia's cheeks flamed now. Without a word she got up from the table, brushing crumbs from the hem of her woollen skirt. She hated the way he persistently ridiculed her relationship with his father, and she longed to throw his words back at him and deny him this favour. But the situation between them was too fragile to precipitate any retaliatory action on his part, and, afraid of her own treacherous feelings, she forced herself to speak collectedly.

'How long does—Miss Eve propose to stay in Chalcott?' she asked stiffly, and Alex looked up at her appraisingly before rising to face her.

'One week, perhaps two,' he remarked carelessly. 'Does it matter?'

'Only to the extent that I should like to give Mrs Winters the full picture,' Olivia replied, uneasily aware of her quickening senses. In black denim jeans and a matching sweat shirt, he was much too disturbing, and avoiding his eyes, she turned towards the door.

'Liv——'

His low use of her name halted her, but she glanced back at him reluctantly, wishing she could be as cool as he was. After all, he was the usurper here, not she, and no matter how justified, he had no right to treat her so outrageously.

'What do you want?' she asked now, and he approached her almost diffidently, one hand massaging the muscles at the back of his neck. The action separated the hem of his shirt from the low waistband of his jeans, exposing a thin line of muscled flesh. That glimpse of brown skin had an hypnotic effect on Olivia, and she thrust her hands behind her back to prevent any involuntary desire to thrust his shirt back into his pants.

'Come with me,' he invited, halting in front of her. 'This afternoon, when I go to pick up Lilian. Come with me!'

Olivia's breathing felt constricted. 'Come with you?' she exclaimed. 'To collect your girl-friend? Why should I?'

'Because I want you to,' he replied softly, removing his hand from the back of his neck and transferring it to her cheek. It was warm and slightly moist, the wetness of his hair—after a shower, she hazarded—providing that trace of dampness on his palm. It was a curiously intimate gesture, the transmittance of moisture from his skin to hers, and she knew a sudden ache in the pit of her stomach, that seemed to spread down, into her thighs.

'Alex——' His name was a protest on her lips, but she seemed rooted to the spot, incapable of either moving or repulsing him.

'Liv,' he responded, with sensual deliberation, and almost against his better judgment, she suspected, he slid his free hand round her waist and pulled her against him. 'No wonder Henry was gulled,' he muttered, the harsh words in plain contradiction of his tongue that was exploring the delicate contours of her ear. 'Even though I know what you are, I can't help wanting you. How's that for irony?'

Olivia didn't resist him. In spite of the outraged cry of her conscience, she let him bring his mouth down upon hers, parting her lips eagerly beneath that hungry abrasion. Without voluntary thought her arms slid round his neck, her fingers threading through the still damp hair at his nape, her body arching towards his with all the unconscious ardour of her untried youth.

'Liv,' he groaned, half in protest, when he felt her body's urgent invitation. His fingers twisted into her hair, entangling themselves in its soft curtain, drawing her closer by its rope of silk. 'Oh, Liv,' he groaned, burying his face in the warm skin of her neck, and for several pulsating seconds they just stood there, wrapped in each other's arms.

At last Alex lifted his head to look down at her with unexpectedly gentle eyes. 'Liv,' he said, lifting one hand and pushing back the hair from her forehead, 'why the hell do I feel as if I'm the offender, when I know you ask for everything you get!'

Olivia drew an unsteady breath. 'And—and what am I asking for?'

'Right now?' His lips twisted. 'Me,' he answered without conceit. 'You want me.' His gaze hardened. 'Which is pretty sickening, considering your husband hasn't been dead above two weeks!'

Olivia tore herself away from him then, unable and unwilling to defend the relationship she had had with Henry. Why should she bare her soul to him? He was only baiting her. Somehow she had to see this through, without losing the shred of self-respect she still possessed.

'He was your father, too,' she reminded him tautly, smoothing the tangled strands of dark hair behind her ears. 'Don't use me to salve your own conscience. Can't you wait until Miss Eve gets here? She's obviously not so exclusive!'

The look he gave her then was belittling, and Olivia turned away from his contemptuous stare. Why did he make her say these things? she asked herself helplessly. She had never been a shrew before. But with him, there was always this sexual conflict, something he was as aware of as she was; and because of that, they were constantly in contention.

The sudden opening of the door behind them gave Olivia a start. The appearance of the maid to clear the table made her realise how reckless their behaviour of a few moments ago had been. If anyone had seen them! If that passionate embrace had become public knowledge! Olivia's legs felt weak at the thought of it, and avoiding Alex's eyes, she made for the door.

'Don't forget we're going out this afternoon.'

Alex's mocking remark gave her pause. 'Going out?' she echoed faintly, casting a nervous glance in the maid's direction.

'Yes. To collect Miss Eve from the hotel,' he remarked, with cool deliberation. 'Don't say you've forgotten. We'll leave about two o'clock.'

Olivia's mouth opened and closed helplessly. What could she say? What excuse could she make, with Julie's ears alert to every intonation in her voice?

Instead of arguing, she paused in the doorway. 'I'll speak to Mrs Winters,' she declared stiffly, without accepting or declining his invitation, and Alex inclined his head lazily as she made her departure.

The housekeeper seemed unperturbed that they were to have two more guests.

'It will do you good, Mrs Gantry,' she exclaimed. 'You need company—young company. And any friend of Master Alex's is bound to be young, isn't she?'

'Yes.' Olivia did not sound enthusiastic, and Mrs Winters clicked her tongue.

'What's the matter, Mrs Gantry?' she asked. 'Are you still not feeling on top form?' She sighed. 'If Master

Alex weren't here, I'd say a holiday was what you needed. A proper holiday, I mean, somewhere nice and warm and sunny. The West Indies, maybe.'

'Or Africa,' remarked Alex behind them, and Olivia turned to see her tormentor leaning indolently against the kitchen door. 'You'd like Tsaba, Liv. Plenty of sunshine there.'

'There you are, then,' said Mrs Winters comfortably. 'Master Alex might take you back to Africa with him. Where was it you said you lived? Gstaad?'

'That's in Switzerland, Mrs Winters,' Alex corrected her drily. 'No—Gstango. It's about fifty miles from the capital.'

'I have no wish to go to Africa, thank you,' Olivia replied icily. 'Mrs Winters, I can leave the arrangements for Mr Gantry's guests in your hands, can't I? I—er—I've got a slight headache. I think I'll go up to my room for a while.'

'Oh, dear!' Mrs Winters was concerned. 'Is there anything I can do?'

'No, nothing, thank you.' Olivia walked towards the door and after a moment's hesitation, Alex stood aside to let her pass. But she was intensely aware of him as she passed his lean hard body, and of the male scent that she had aroused.

Nevertheless, despite the fact that her head was aching rather badly by the time she reached her room, Olivia did not lie down. She was too tense to relax, too physically and emotionally overwrought to consider any alternative to movement. She could not sit still, and she paced the soft carpet in mild desperation.

Somehow she had to come to some decision about the future. What did she intend to do if—and this was the crux of the matter—if Alex became chairman of the Gantry corporation? She could not continue to live in the same house as him, that was obvious. But what would he do once he was told of her suggestion? Would her decision alleviate the hostility between them? Did she want it to? For she knew that a prolonged relationship with Alex Gantry could have only one conclusion . . .

She paced restlessly to the windows, gripping the curtain tightly and staring out into the fountain that rippled coolly in the courtyard. It was a crisp morning, the sun making a gallant effort to displace the misty clouds that rose from the hedgerows. It was the kind of day she loved, a day when, if Henry were still alive, she would have gone walking along by the river, squelching through the water meadows, and watching the birds building their nests. But now the river was forever tinged with the sadness of Alex's mother's death, and the plans she had made so naïvely, to sell off Henry's empire and give the money to charity, were all as futile as her feelings for Alex.

She sighed. If only there were someone she could talk to, someone she could share her feelings with. Everything seemed to be working against her: from Henry's careful planning for the corporation's future, to her own mother's involvement with Alex's father. Had she known? Had her mother known what had happened to Mrs Gantry? Had she realised that her trivial affair had caused the deaths of two people, not one? And how could she, Olivia, be expected to punish Henry's son for something for which he had already suffered punishment enough? No, she only had one course: that of giving Alex back what was rightfully his, and then disappearing completely out of his life.

Lunch was at one, and when she went downstairs she felt more equipped to deal with the situation. She had taken a couple of aspirin, showered, and changed into a slim-fitting cream dress, with wide sleeves that ended in a neat cuff, and a fringed hem. Her long hair was secured in a tight knot on top of her head, and the severity of the style softened her features and gave an upward tilt to her eyes that was most becoming, had she but known it. She felt she looked calm and collected, an appearance that was belied by the sudden quickening of her pulses when she found Alex waiting for her.

He, too, had changed his clothes, and the wine-coloured corded suit and white shirt accentuated the streaked paleness of his hair. The close-fitting pants did little to disguise the lean muscularity of his hips, and the open neck of his shirt revealed the fine chain of the medallion she had noticed before.

Because Julie was waiting to serve the meal, conversation was limited to impersonal issues, but Alex's eyes, dark and disturbing, held an unmistakable message. They tore away the serenity she was struggling to uphold, piercing the shield of her resistance and reducing her defences to a crumbling shell. Just by looking at her as he was doing, he could make her doubt the fundamental barriers of their relationship, and contempt for her own weakness once more hardened her attitude towards him.

'I phoned Lilian,' he remarked, unfolding his table napkin, and after an involuntary glance at Julie's departing back, Olivia shrugged.

'So?'

'So—she's looking forward to meeting you.'

Olivia sighed. 'You can't be serious!'

'Why not? You may like her. Have you considered that?'

Olivia picked up her soup spoon. 'Whether or not I like her is hardly relevant,' she declared, determinedly tasting the spicy dish of minestrone Julie had set in front of her.

'Liv!' His tone was impatient. 'At least give her the benefit of the doubt, hmm? She's a nice girl.'

'Is that your opinion?'

'Yes.'

Olivia made no response to this and for a while they ate in silence. But then, after Julie had taken the soup plates away and put dishes containing meat and vegetables on the table, he said:

'I meant to ask you: you went to see Adam Cosgrove yesterday. Why? What did he want?'

Olivia's lips parted. 'You have a nerve!'

'No. Just an interest.' His eyes challenged hers. 'Did he speak about me?'

'Olivia hesitated. 'He—he told me how your mother died, actually. I never knew.'

'I see.' Alex considered her reply. 'And what was your reaction?'

'I was shocked, naturally.' Olivia moved her shoulders. 'I can understand why you're so bitter.'

'Can you?' Alex made a derisive sound. 'It's a little late for that, isn't it?'

Olivia held up her head. 'Not necessarily.'

'You mean you're going to hand the estate back to me, on a plate!'

'I can't do that.'

'No, I don't suppose you can,' he remarked caustically.

Olivia was stung by his tone. 'That's not to say I wouldn't want to,' she declared recklessly, ignoring Adam's advice. 'I don't want Henry's money. I never did.'

'So why did you marry him?' Alex was contemptuous.

Olivia opened her mouth to tell him, then closed it again. How could she? she realised with horror. How could she explain her reasons for marrying Henry to his son? Particularly when her mother's affair with his father was the sole reason she and not Alex had control of the estate!

'Well?' Alex taunted. 'It isn't the first time I've asked you. You've had plenty of time to think of an answer. You don't marry someone without a reason, and somehow I find your protestations of hatred a little hard to swallow.'

'I don't have to answer you,' exclaimed Olivia hotly. 'You father asked me to marry him and I accepted. You can make what you like of it.'

Alex propped his chin on one hand. 'But if you didn't want his money and you hated him——' He shook his head. 'You must have wanted something from him. What was it—revenge?'

Olivia forced herself to meet his dark gaze with grim determination. If she showed any dismay, he would know he was on the right track, and he was the kind of man who would pursue it to the bitter end.

'I think you're allowing your imagination to run away with you,' she said tautly. 'Eat your lunch. You don't want to keep Miss Eve waiting.'

'No, we don't, do we?' he retorted, and Olivia decided it was easier not to argue.

After Julie had served the coffee to finish the meal, Alex rose to his feet. 'Are you ready?' he asked, thrusting his hands into his jacket pockets, and Olivia had, perforce, to look up at him.

'Am I ready?'

Alex sighed. 'Would you prefer it if we spent the afternoon pursuing your reasons for marrying my father?'

Olivia's nails curled into her palms. 'Is that a threat?'

'Just a promise,' he replied evenly. 'Relax, Liv. I won't expose your petty reasons. If they justify what you did to you, why should I destroy them? Besides,' his gaze moved insolently over her breasts, 'I've no doubt you consider you paid for the privilege of calling yourself Mrs Henry Gantry!'

Olivia rose to her feet. 'You are——'

'—despicable?' He shrugged. 'I know. You've told me. Now, get your coat, like a good girl, and meet me in the hall.'

Olivia walked out of the room, determined not to obey him. But something, some quirk of fate, made her glance back. Alex was standing where she had left him, staring broodingly out of the window now, and as she watched, he ran both hands over his scalp to grip the hair at the back of his neck. It was a curiously defeated gesture, and for a moment she knew a quite ridiculous desire to comfort him. But Alex Gantry did not need her sympathy, she thought, climbing the shallow steps to the entrance hall, and after Mary had collected her fur jacket from her room and slipped it about her shoulders, she despised the sudden weakening that had made her give in to his demands.

The Maserati was waiting at the door by the time Alex joined her. He had not troubled to put on a coat and Olivia, aware of the chilly air outside, was obliged to suggest that he might find an open-necked shirt and jacket rather inadequate.

'The car's warm,' he remarked, putting a hand beneath her elbow to guide her outside, and her skin prickled even through the thickness of her sleeve. 'But I'm touched that you care.'

'I don't want another cold,' Olivia retorted shortly, but his complacent smile revealed his disbelief in this statement.

All the same he was right. The Maserati's heater soon dealt with the cool air and Olivia relaxed in her seat as the security guard closed the gates behind them.

'Some castle,' observed Alex, glancing back over his shoulder. 'The Bank of England can't be better protected!'

'You didn't seem to find the walls too difficult to scale,' she responded, and he smiled.

'I guess I knew all the right passwords, hmm?' he suggested, and Olivia glanced quickly at him.

'You used to live here, didn't you?'

Alex's eyes narrowed. 'Is that a serious question?'

'No.' Olivia shook her head. 'No.' She looked out of the window. 'Where are we going?'

'Chalcott.'

'Chalcott?' She stared at him. 'You mean—this girl has been staying in Chalcott since you came here?'

'No.' Alex shook his head now. 'As a matter of fact, since she arrived in England two weeks ago she's been staying with some friends in London.'

'And the boy?'

'What boy?'

'Her son!'

'Oh—yes.' Alex hunched his shoulders. 'Him, too.'

Olivia frowned. 'Did—did she come back from Africa with you?'

Alex sighed. 'Not with me. But she has been living in Africa, yes.'

'In Tsaba?'

'Yes.'

'In that place you mentioned—what was it? Gstango?'

Alex nodded. 'She's a nurse. She worked at the hospital there.'

'Is she English?'

'South African, actually,' replied Alex shortly. 'This is some inquisition! I thought you weren't interested.'

'If she's going to be staying at the house, I should

know something about her,' exclaimed Olivia defensively.

'You will.' Alex spoke flatly. 'Here's the hotel. Do you want to come in with me or wait here?'

'I—I'll wait.'

'Okay.'

Alex vaulted out of the car, and she watched him walk into the hotel. He moved with a lithe easy stride, indicative of the energetic life he had led. She thought of Henry, prematurely aged by the constant struggle to increase his fortune, a fortune he could neither spend nor dispose of in his lifetime, and knew a fleeting sympathy for the waste of human relationships. If Alex had been more understanding; if Henry had been more forgiving; but how could she condemn either one when she had so much to reproach herself with?

A movement near the entrance of the hotel attracted her attention and glancing round she saw the toddler and his mother she had seen in the park the previous afternoon. She recognised the child's fleecy jump-suit and the young woman's distinctive auburn hair, and she was about to smile a greeting when a man came out of the hotel behind them, carrying two suitcases.

It was Alex, and even as she watched he spoke to the young woman with the easy familiarity of long association. Oh God! Olivia thought, swinging round in her seat with a distinctly sick feeling. No wonder she had thought the child looked like Alex! It was his! It was his son. And the young woman, this Lilian Eve, was not his girl-friend or his mistress; she was his wife!

But no! That couldn't be so, unless Alex was lying. He had insisted she wasn't married. So what was she? His common-law wife? Did they have such things in South Africa? Or were they simply living together?

Olivia was in a state of some agitation by the time Alex swung open his door and lifted the small boy into the back of the car. 'Here we are,' he remarked unnecessarily, drawing the young woman forward. 'Allow me to introduce you. Liv, this is Lilian; Lilian, meet Mrs Gantry. Mrs Henry Gantry!' He made a careless gesture. 'Sorry if we've kept you waiting.'

CHAPTER EIGHT

OLIVIA could only move her head in a negative gesture, but Lilian Eve had no such misgivings. 'I'm so pleased to meet you, Mrs Gantry,' she exclaimed, taking the rather limp hand Olivia offered her as she climbed into the back beside her son. 'And this is Sacha. Sacha, say hello to the lady. He's a bit of a handful,' she added apologetically, 'but I'll try and keep him out of your way.'

'Oh, I—there's no need.' Olivia made a determined effort to be civil. She could not take her resentment out on the child. 'Hello, Sacha. How old are you?'

'He's nearly two,' replied Alex, having disposed of the cases and a folding pushchair into the boot, and levering himself behind the wheel beside her. His eyes held hers with careless arrogance. 'He's a handsome little fellow, isn't he? And quite a handful, as Lilian says.'

'You would know,' said Olivia, between tight lips, and Alex's mouth twisted.

'Would I?'

'He looks like you,' retorted Olivia almost inaudibly, under cover of his starting the car.

'Does he?' Alex glanced behind him before pulling out into the stream of traffic. 'I'll take that as a compliment, however it was meant.'

'Why didn't you tell me?' she demanded impassionedly, as Lilian pointed out some horses and their riders to the small boy, and Alex gave her an aggravating look.

'Tell you? Tell you what?' he responded. 'I didn't

think it would matter to you what the boy looked like.'

Olivia's jaw ached with the pressure she was putting upon it. 'You're deliberately misunderstanding me,' she hissed. 'What I can't understand is why you have to lie about it!'

'I've told you no lies about Sacha,' he retorted flatly. Then, casting a look over his shoulder, he said: 'You're going to like staying with Mrs Gantry, Sacha. She has plenty of room for you to play.'

Mrs Winters was waiting when they arrived back at the house, and her eyes widened with delight when she saw the little boy.

'Well, and isn't he just the image of what Master Alex was when he was little more than a baby!' she announced, seemingly unconcerned at the ambiguity of her remark. 'Come along with me, Master Sacha, and we'll find some milk and biscuits, hmm?'

Lilian glanced at Alex, and he nodded. 'Let him go with Mrs Winters,' he said easily. 'She'll look after him while we have tea with Mrs Gantry.'

Olivia could hardly evade that pointed reminder of her hostess duties, and after giving the housekeeper her instructions, she led the way into the small drawing room.

'Won't you sit down, Mrs—*Miss* Eve?' she suggested, indicating one of the soft velvet sofas that faced one another across a wide hearth. Although the room was small compared to others in the house, it was still of generous proportions, and with Alex and Miss Eve on one side of the hearth and herself on the other, she felt she would be more able to cope with the situation.

But although Lilian seated herself on the sofa she had indicated, Alex chose to join Olivia, stretching his length on the cushioned seat beside her, deliberately, she was sure, leaving only an inch of space between them. It was disturbing and embarrassing, particularly with Lilian watching their every move, and she wondered if it was a deliberate attempt to show the other girl he still had no intention of marrying her.

'You have a lovely home, Mrs Gantry,' Lilian exclaimed, while Olivia was endeavouring to come to terms with this latest development. 'This is a beautiful room. And what a wonderful view!'

'Yes.' Olivia's tongue circled her upper lip. 'We—we are very fortunate.' She paused. 'I understand you're a South African.'

'I was born there,' Lilian nodded. 'In Cape Town. I did my nursing training there, but after I'd qualified, I moved away. First to Zambia, and then later to Tsaba.'

'Where—er——' Olivia glanced at Alex, 'where you met my—stepson.'

'Yes.'

Lilian agreed, but she seemed a little uneasy now, and while her eyes darted nervously about the room, Olivia exchanged a look with the man beside her. Alex did not seem at all perturbed, however, and his arm along the cushion behind her was much too close for comfort.

'Have you been to England before, Miss Eve?' she ventured, wanting to ask about Sacha, but incapable of doing so, and the other girl returned her gaze with evident relief, obviously glad not to be asked any more pointed question.

'No,' she said now. 'This is my first visit. But I like it. It—it's civilised.'

'Isn't it, though,' remarked Alex, half under his breath, and Olivia knew the strongest impulse to call his bluff there and then. But to do so would be to expose Lilian, as well as himself, and Olivia found she was developing a liking for the girl.

Mrs Winters brought the tea trolley herself, chuckling when Alex asked what Sacha was doing. 'He's got Mr Murdoch playing pick-a-back round the kitchen,' she declared, smiling at Olivia's surprise. 'Yes, I was as astounded as you were, Mrs Gantry. I never thought to see that man lose his dignity.'

'I hope he's not being a nuisance,' Lilian murmured doubtfully, as Mrs Winters quickly shook her head.

'Bless you, no. We're all delighted to have a baby in the house again. When—well, when your father married Miss Olivia, Master Alex, we thought—I hope I'm not speaking out of place, but—well, we thought there might be another baby before too long. Of course, it was not to be, and in the circumstances, perhaps it was just as well, but now——' She gave Olivia an apologetic look. 'Young Sacha makes us feel young again. Like when Master Alex was a baby.'

Lilian turned anxious eyes in Olivia's direction, and Olivia guessed she was apprehensive of her reaction. For her own part, she didn't know which was the stronger emotion—embarrassment or compassion. She had never imagined Mrs Winters and the other members of the staff might expect her and Henry to start a family of their own. Their relationship had been so different from what anyone imagined, and there had never been any question of children. As for Lilian, she must be living in constant fear of her association with Alex being discovered, for how could she sustain any credibility here if their real relationship was revealed? But why hadn't he married her? He obviously cared for the boy, or he would never have suggested bringing him to England. What was he trying to do, get the child away from its mother? Or did he intend to use Sacha to further his own claims to the Gantry estate?

'After you've had tea, shall I show Miss Eve where she and the little one are going to sleep, Mrs Gantry?' Mrs Winters added, when Olivia made no immediate response, but before she could respond, Alex forestalled her.

'No, I'll do that, Mrs Winters,' he averred easily. 'The suite overlooking the swimming pool, didn't you say?'

'That's right.' Mrs Winters seemed relieved that at least he had not taken offence at her familiarity. 'Is that all right, Mrs Gantry? You've got everything you need?'

'Thank you, Mrs Winters.' Olivia forced a smile to show she was not displeased. 'I'm sure we're all going to benefit from Sacha's arrival.'

'Yes, Mrs Gantry.' Mrs Winters was definitely easier now, and with a final twitch of the traycloth, she made a thankful departure.

Olivia was obliged to serve tea, which wasn't made easier when Alex moved forward on the couch, too, his thigh brushing familiarly against her leg. 'Cream—cream and sugar, Miss Eve?' she asked, as Alex's breath fanned her cheek, and Lilian leant to take her cup with endearing eagerness.

'Thank you,' she said, accepting a smoked salmon sandwich as well. 'Hmm, these are gorgeous! I think smoked salmon is my most favourite food!'

Olivia's smile was strained, particularly when she gave Alex his cup and his lean fingers touched hers with deliberate intimacy. God, what was he trying to do? she thought, staring at him in helpless indignation, but Alex's expression never wavered, his careless mockery only evident in his eyes.

'You've got a loose hair—just there,' he said, his fingers lingering against her neck longer than was necessary to remove the errant strand. 'You smell delicious,' he added, for her ears only, and the wave of warm colour that swept up her face was totally uncontrollable.

Lilian seemed undisturbed by this exchange, however, and Olivia felt a hopeless sense of bewilderment. The boy was Henry's grandson, he *had* to be! And yet Lilian was acting as if she was completely indifferent to Alex's behaviour. Didn't she care? Was that why they had never got married, because she didn't care about him? And was Alex using her to make Lilian jealous, instead of the other way about?

She was utterly relieved when tea was over and Alex rose lithely to his feet. 'Come along, Lilian,' he said, holding out his hand to help her up. 'It's time for Cinderella to see the rest of the palace!'

'Oh, *Leon!*'

Lilian spoke carelessly, releasing herself from his grasp as soon as she was on her feet and punching him lightly on the arm. But then she seemed to realise exactly what she had said, and with hot colour darkening her cheeks now, she cast an anxious look in Olivia's direction.

'I—er—I always call—Alex—Leon,' she offered feebly. 'It—er—it's my name for him.'

Olivia gave a tight smile. 'Don't mind me. I have private names for him myself.'

'And I you,' Alex countered lazily. 'Come on, Lilian, let me show you how the other half lives.'

Olivia did not see either of them again before dinner. After Julie had cleared the trolley away, she decided it was too late to take the walk she would have liked, to clear her head, and instead she made her way to Henry's study, and attended to some of the correspondence which had piled up while she was unwell. As Henry Gantry's wife, she was expected to contribute to various charities, and there were matters concerning the estate to be dealt with, which she would have to discuss with Francis next time she saw him.

Thinking of Francis, she wondered how he would view her latest action. She could not believe he would approve of her allowing Alex to bring another woman into the house, and when he saw Sacha he could not fail to see the resemblance, as she had done.

Sacha, she thought with a frown. It was an unusual name for a boy. But then she remembered: Sacha was often used as a diminutive form of Alexander. Surely proof indeed of the child's identity!

Dinner was not an easy meal. Lilian was clearly nervous, while Olivia found it was incredibly difficult to avoid controversial subjects. Alex, for his part, contributed little to the conversation, and although his eyes still held a challenge when they encountered Olivia's, he seemed content to keep silent and avoid open conflict.

When the meal was over, Lilian excused herself to go and see if Sacha had settled down, and Olivia would have followed her out of the room had Alex not intercepted her at the door.

'Don't go,' he said. 'I want to talk to you. Shall we go into the study? We can have privacy there.'

Olivia stiffened her spine. 'Why don't you go and talk to your son? Isn't he more deserving of your time? And the child's mother: I'm sure she would appreciate your attentions more than I would.'

'I doubt it,' he retorted brusquely, his fingers around her wrist loose, but as secure as a manacle. 'Now stop playing games and lead the way into the study. I don't want to have to drag you there. That might cause some comment.'

Olivia seethed. 'Tell me what you want here. Whatever it is can't be that important!'

'Oh, but it is.' Alex fixed a smile on his face as the

maid appeared to clear the table. 'Now, where did you say those papers were, Liv? In the study?'

She had to go with him, but she refused to look at him when they were safely within the walls of the study, with the door sealed tightly behind them. Instead, she stood stiffly, waiting for him to proceed, and to her annoyance, he circled the desk and seated himself in Henry's chair.

'Now, isn't this nice?' he remarked, tipping the chair back on its rear legs and propping his feet on the desk. 'But please, won't you sit down? You're making me nervous standing there.'

'I doubt if anything could make *you* nervous!' retorted Olivia hotly. 'You have the unhappy knack of always saying the wrong thing. I can't imagine what you have to say to me that warrants this measure of secrecy, but I wish you'd say it and get to the point of this unnecessary exhibition.'

'An unnecessary exhibition, hmm?' Alex's dark face sobered and he dropped his feet to the floor. 'Very well, *Mrs* Gantry,' his lips twisted, 'did you marry Henry knowing he suspected you were his daughter?'

'His daughter!'

Olivia's lips formed the words, but they were scarcely uttered.

'That's what I said,' agreed Alex flatly. 'Were you aware that he had that suspicion?'

'No!' The word was torn from her. 'No. What are you saying? Henry was not my father. My—my father died nearly twenty years ago. Oh——' her face constricted painfully, 'how—how can you say it? How can you suggest such a thing? I—I don't know where you got that information——'

'I got it from a woman called Stone—Drusilla Stone. Do you know her?'

Olivia groped for a chair and sank into it weakly.

'Mrs—Mrs Stone?' she echoed. 'Yes. Yes, I know her. She—she was a friend of Henry's.'

'A close friend, or so she told me,' inserted Alex evenly.

'She was his mistress,' said Olivia blankly, too shocked to hold anything back. But then the horror of what Alex was suggesting washed over her again, and she put both hands to her head, as if it was in danger of detaching itself from her body.

'I'm sorry you had to hear it so baldly,' he remarked, as she endeavoured to calm herself. 'But you did ask me to come to the point——'

'And you *enjoyed* doing so,' she accused him tremulously. 'My God! The depths to which people will sink, just for the sake of money! I didn't want your father's money, I told you that! And if Drusilla Stone thinks she can go around making those kind of insinuations——'

'I don't think it was an insinuation,' Alex interrupted her narrowly. 'I think she believes it. And I think that perhaps Henry believed it, too.'

'What are you saying?' Olivia stared at him with horrified eyes.

'I'm only repeating what she told me.'

'And Drusilla Stone hates me!'

'Well, let's face it, she has no reason to love you,' Alex exclaimed impatiently. 'You did deprive her of her most valued client.'

'You're disgusting!'

'No, I'm practical. Come on, Liv! You know what Drusilla Stone was—*is*! She wants to hurt you, but she knows there would be no point in making up a lie.'

'Did—did she tell you about my mother and—and your father?'

'She said your mother was the other woman, yes.'

Olivia's features felt frozen. 'The—the woman who was responsible for your mother committing suicide,' she said bitterly.

'Not necessarily.' Alex made an offhand gesture. 'Let's be completely honest, your mother might not have been the only woman in Henry's life.'

'Don't patronise me,' exclaimed Olivia coldly. 'You must know perfectly well they were having an affair. Why else—why else did you suggest what you did?'

Alex frowned. 'Liv, I simply wanted to know what your position was. Whether you married Henry believing it was the only way to secure your inheritance.'

Olivia gasped. 'I wouldn't do that!'

'No.' Alex pushed back his chair and got to his feet. 'No, I'm beginning to believe you wouldn't. So where does that leave us?'

'Nowhere. It leaves us nowhere.' Olivia was too distraught to listen to him. 'I just hope you're satisfied, that's all. You've succeeded in destroying any shred of decency I might have left. I didn't want to marry your father. I did it because my mother was dying and it was what she wanted. But Drusilla was right about one thing—I do wish I'd never set eyes on any of the Gantrys!'

'Liv!'

He came towards her then, his expression half impatient, half cajoling, but Olivia didn't wait to hear whatever else he had to say. With a little sob, she whirled on her heels and rushed towards the door, and the sound of it banging behind her echoed hollowly around the halls as she sped up the stairs to her room.

Behind closed, and locked, doors, she sank down on to the bed, crying weakly. It was horrible, so horrible she could hardly bear to think about it, but she knew

she would have to think about it, and about the im-
plications that it raised.

Henry could not have believed she was his daughter,
could he? It wasn't true. It couldn't be true! Her father
had been Andrew Powell. He was the son of another
Andrew Powell, the founder of Powell Pharmaceuticals.
She had been born in Croydon, in the Victorian house
in Hargrave Street where she and her parents had lived
until Mr Powell's death in 1959. She had had no association with Henry Gantry, she had not even known of
his identity until she was sixteen, when her mother had
confided the whole story to her. It didn't make any
sense, what Alex had told her. And besides, the coincidence was too great. Why should Henry have waited so
long before coming to see her mother? And if he had
suspected their relationship, surely there were other
ways he could have claimed her as his daughter.

But were there? As she sat there, staring bewilderedly
at her own reflection, she was forced to concede that by
marrying her, he had secured her future far more effec-
tively than any other method could have done. After
all, he was pushed for time. He knew he was dying, and
the effort of going to court and proving their relationship might have taken too long, or been too much
for him. He had not been a well man, she had known
that. From the very beginning, he had had to take each
day carefully, caring for his health in a way she had
known was abhorrent to him.

But they had never become close, as they surely would
have done if he had announced she was his daughter,
she thought painfully. Indeed, in some ways they had
remained strangers, right up until the end. Perhaps that
had been her fault. Perhaps, because she had found it
hard to forgive his treatment of the man she still believed
to be her father, she had held herself apart from any
sense of intimacy, and although, in public, they had

presented a united front, in private their lives had been detached, separate.

She sighed wearily, getting up from the bed and walking closer to the mirror. Her reflection gazed back at her, pale and hollow-eyed, the stains her tears had left on her cheeks adding to her wan appearance. Dear God, she breathed, there was no resemblance there, was there? She and Alex could not—*must not*—be sister and brother! It simply could not be true!

Someone tapping at her door alerted her to the fact that it was still early, barely half past nine. It was probably Mary, she thought, moving away from the glass. She couldn't face her now. Not when she would expect an explanation why Olivia's evening should have ended in tears.

'Who—who is it?' she called, unable to keep the tremor out of her voice, and then clasped her hands tightly together as Alex's low voice answered her:

'It's me, Liv. Open the door. We still have things to discuss.'

'Go away!' Olivia made no move towards the door, remaining where she was, like a statue, frozen in an attitude of revulsion.

'Liv——'

'I said go away,' she repeated huskily. 'Please—leave me alone!'

'For God's sake!' Alex swore violently, and she heard as well as saw the handle turn beneath his hand. 'Come on, Liv! Open this door! Or do you want me to break it down?'

'You wouldn't do that.' Olivia moved then, hurrying towards the door and pressing herself against it, almost as if her paltry weight would prevent what keys and locks could not. 'Alex, don't make a scene, please! We—we'll talk again in the morning.'

'Tonight,' he said heavily, rattling the handle again.

'Liv, playing for time isn't going to help anything. We have to talk this out together.'

'We have nothing to talk out!' Olivia was getting hysterical. 'Go away, Alex! Go away! Go back to your *family*. Leave me alone!'

It was fully fifteen minutes before she really believed he had gone. Even then, she left the door half reluctantly, as if afraid by doing so, she was abandoning her defences. But nothing happened. There was no further sound beyond the elegantly panelled doors, and with a feeling of despair comparable to nothing she had ever experienced, she slowly prepared for bed.

The telephone rang as she was climbing into bed, but she ignored it. She would not put it past Alex to try and contact her this way when all other ways had failed, and when another tap came at her door, she stiffened instinctively.

'Yes?' she called, realising it could be one of the servants, and was relieved when Mary Parrish called:

'It's Mr Kennedy, Mrs Gantry. He's on the phone, and he wants to speak to you. Shall I put him through?'

'Francis?' Olivia's shoulders sagged. 'Oh, yes, I'll speak to him, Mary. I'll take it here.'

'Yes, Mrs Gantry.'

Mary went away and a few moments later Olivia picked up her receiver to hear Francis' calm, and somehow reassuring, voice.

'Mrs Gantry?' He paused a moment for her to answer him. 'Oh, Mrs Gantry, I hope I'm not ringing too late.'

'Not at all, Francis.' Olivia adjusted the strap of her nightgown. 'Was it something urgent?'

'Well, you might think so, Mrs Gantry.' Francis sounded concerned. 'Your—er—your stepson was seen having a drink with Mrs Stone earlier this evening.'

How quickly news carried in a small town, thought Olivia tautly, dreading what was to come next. But realising Francis was waiting for some response from her, she decided to be honest.

'I know,' she said, evidently surprising Francis by her answer. 'Er—Alex told me he'd seen her.'

'Did he?' Francis sounded almost disappointed at having been forestalled. 'Oh, then you'll know of the enquiries he's been making; how he's been digging up all the gossip about Henry's past!'

Olivia's fingers tightened around the receiver. 'I—I imagine he feels some sense of resentment towards his father for—for what happened to his mother.'

'You know about that?'

'Adam Cosgrove told me.'

'I see.' Francis hesitated. 'Well, we've been doing a little enquiring of our own, and it isn't altogether certain that he is who he says he is.'

'Alex?' Olivia swallowed convulsively.

'Alex, yes.'

'But—I thought you knew him——'

'I did. But he was only a boy when he left England, not much more than seventeen. A man can change a lot in fifteen years.'

Olivia's legs were trembling. 'But—but why should you be suspicious?'

'My dear Mrs Gantry, we can't afford to make any mistakes. Not if you're considering appointing him in his father's place.'

'No. No, I suppose not.' Olivia shook her head blankly. 'But how long are these enquiries likely to take?'

'That I can't say.' Francis was apologetic. 'Tsaba isn't exactly round the corner, you know, Mrs Gantry.'

'But surely you have someone——'

'Oh, yes. We have an agent in Zambia, and he's been assigned to the job, but judging by the call I had from him this afternoon, I'd say he wasn't meeting with a great deal of success.'

'Why not?' Olivia was tense. 'Francis, surely it's only a matter of speaking to people who know him—people who worked with him.'

'I get the impression they're not exactly willing to co-operate.'

'But why?'

'Mrs Gantry, these people were his friends, his colleagues. I don't think they trust anyone coming and asking personal questions.'

'But that's ridiculous!' Olivia moved her head helplessly. 'Francis, are you sure this man is doing everything he can to get this information?'

Francis sounded hurt. 'Don't you trust me, Mrs Gantry?'

'Of course I do, Francis, but I want this information. I want to know.'

'Don't we all!'

Olivia pressed her lips together, and then came to a sudden decision. 'We'll go,' she said. 'You and I together. We'll find out whether this man is Alex Gantry, or an impostor.'

Francis gasped, 'You have to be crazy!'

'Why?'

'Well, I can't just abandon my job——'

'Don't you have a deputy?'

'Well—yes, but——' Francis broke off. 'Mrs Gantry, are you aware this is the rainy season in Tsaba?'

'Does that matter?'

'Does it matter?' Francis spluttered. 'Mrs Gantry, there are no motorways in Tsaba—at least, not so you'd notice. The roads are deplorable in places. Can you imagine what it must be like, getting around in the rainy season?'

'I expect we'd manage.'

Olivia refused to be deterred. For the first time since Henry's death, she felt her life had some motivation. Whatever Francis said, she would go to Tsaba. It was what she needed—action. And what she wanted, too. To know the truth, once and for all. Whatever the truth about her parentage, she had to find out whether Alex was telling the truth about his own. And, incidentally, to discover whether the feelings for him which were tearing her apart were forbidden by law—or providence.

CHAPTER NINE

THE Mission at Bakoua was hot, hotter than anything Olivia could have imagined. There was no air-conditioning, and in the heat of the day the temperature soared well above a hundred degrees. Even Pastor Schmitt and his wife rested after lunch, and only Olivia's driving determination kept her from flaking out on the narrow iron bed, where she had spent the previous night. Instead, she was seated on a cushioned lounger on the verandah, waiting for the arrival of the jeep which was to take her and Francis to the small mining community of Gstango.

It was three days since they had arrived in Tsaba. At first, landing at the streamlined airport and driving into the country's capital of Ashenghi, Olivia had been seduced into thinking Francis had exaggerated the difficulties. But after taking two days to cover a distance which should have been covered in as many hours, she had rapidly revised that opinion.

The journey had been terrible. The muddy tracks they called roads had been swamplike and almost unnegotiable; they had been tossed about like sacks of straw in vehicles whose springs were distinctly suspect, and bitten to death by swarms of insects, rising from the undergrowth after every downpour. And when it rained, it really rained. Olivia had never seen water pouring from the sky in such quantities, and although it was blessedly cool while it was falling, it was damnably humid after.

There were times when she had, admittedly, regretted embarking on this journey. Times when the heat had made her skin feel as if it was crawling with a hundred

144

insects, or when the perspiration pouring from her body uncomfortably dampened her clothes. But in the main, she tried not to be downhearted, discovering within herself a determination she had not known she possessed. Whatever happened, it was better than sitting at home, living in apprehension of what Francis' agent might or might not find out. She was here, she was involved; and no matter how ill-advised her motivation, she was within fifteen miles of her objective.

There hadn't been much time during the past three days to wonder what Alex's reactions to her departure had been. Indeed, she had not seen him since that scene in Henry's study, but after what Francis had told her, she had no doubt he had plenty to occupy his time. The morning after that unfortunate scene, he had left the house before breakfast, and it had been left to Olivia to share an uncomfortable hour with Lilian and the baby before having Forsyth drive her to the airport, where she had arranged to meet Francis.

It had all been planned the night before. The West African Airlines flight left at midday, and much against his better judgement, Francis had booked two seats on it. He had muttered all the way to Zurich about medical certificates and inoculations against cholera and sleeping sickness, but as no mandatory health requirements had been necessary, Olivia had waived these considerations. Her primary concern was to reach Tsaba before Alex learned what she was doing and took steps to forbid her, although how he could actually do that, she was not absolutely sure.

Nevertheless, eating breakfast that morning with Lilian and the baby, she had been made acutely aware of the ambiguity of her position. If she had married Henry for his money, if she had been the gold-digger Alex had believed her to be, the situation might never have developed. As it was, she had only herself to blame for allowing him to bring the child and its mother to the house, and now that they were there, she couldn't help but feel that their rights were stronger than hers.

After all, Alex was Henry's son, and Sacha was evidently Alex's son. Even Henry had not ruled out the possibility of that development, and the provisions of the will covered this contingency. But Henry had not known he already had a grandson, or that Olivia would be foolish enough to feel sympathy for Alex.

The sound of someone moving behind her made Olivia glance round now to see Francis coming through the french doors, scratching his head. The heat did not agree with him, that much was obvious, and his fair skin had an unhealthy sheen, the growth of his beard the only colour in his face.

'Do you want some orange juice?' Olivia suggested, getting to her feet and eyeing him sympathetically. 'Oh, Francis, you do look pale. Didn't you get any sleep?'

'In there?' Francis cast a sceptical look over his shoulder. 'Have you any idea what the temperature is in my room?' He snorted derisively. 'Room! I should say my cell, my *cubicle*; the twenty-four square feet I can call my own!'

'Sit down.' Olivia invited him to take her chair, and poured some of the wilting orange juice into a glass. The ice it had contained had long melted, but at least it was cool and refreshing. 'Here, drink this,' she said. 'It will make you feel better.'

Francis took the chair she offered and gulped the orange juice greedily. Watching him, Olivia was concerned for his appearance. He really was not reacting at all well to these conditions, and she was very much afraid he wasn't fit to drive the last fifteen miles to Gstango.

'God! What a place!' he muttered, setting down the empty glass on the table. 'Who would choose to live here? They must be out of their tiny minds!'

'It is hot,' agreed Olivia, fanning herself with a languid hand. In cream cotton shirt and pants, she didn't think there was an inch of flesh where her clothes were not sticking to her, but unlike Francis, she was invigorated by the challenge.

'Hot! It's the fiery furnace!' declared Francis, tipping his head back wearily. 'Hell must be something like this, only cooler.'

Olivia's smile was apologetic. 'I'm sorry, Francis, I shouldn't have brought you here. It's obvious you're finding it a lot harder to stand than me. I should have come on my own. I shouldn't have involved you.'

'Hey ...' Francis gave her a wry look, 'I'm the one who's supposed to make those kind of statements. Me, the macho male!' He grimaced. 'Some macho male, I am. Here we are, miles from civilisation, and instead of thinking: me, Tarzan, you, Jane, I'm flaking out at the first hurdle.'

Olivia hesitated, and then put slightly damp fingers against his forehead. It was burning up, and her sense of responsibility deepened as she realised he really wasn't at all well.

'I think you should stay here, Francis,' she said propping her back against one of the wooden struts that supported the verandah. 'It would be crazy for you to venture any farther into the bush. I think you've got a fever.'

Francis' brows descended. 'You're not serious! Do you think I'd allow you to disappear into the jungle with strangers!'

Olivia sighed. 'I know how you feel, Francis, and it's sweet of you to be concerned about me, but really, I'm not as helpless as I look.'

'Aren't you?' Francis was disbelieving. 'Who was it who nearly had hysterics at the hotel in Ashenghi, when she found a spider in the wardrobe?'

'That was different.' Olivia was impatient. 'I just don't
like spiders, that's all.'

'And don't you think there'll be spiders at Gstango?
And lizards, and other crawling insects——'

'Oh, stop it!' Olivia shuddered and moved away from
the verandah rail, just in case some other form of insect
life should choose to take advantage of the unbuttoned
neckline of her shirt. 'I'd manage, Francis, honestly.
And—and I'd feel better if you were at least resting
here.'

'Well, forget it.' Francis was determined, too. 'When
the jeep arrives, I'll be ready. I'm not letting you out of
my sight until we get back to England.'

Olivia shrugged, and as she did so, she heard the
unmistakeable sound of a vehicle approaching. It was
difficult to see anything through the heavy belt of trees
that formed a barrier round the small compound, but
presently the jeep burst from the bush and came to an
abrupt halt in front of the mission, its tyres throwing up
a flurry of pebbles.

It was an open-topped vehicle, and Olivia was glad
the sun was beginning its swift descent into oblivion. At
least in darkness they would not be troubled by its
overwhelming glare, even if the mosquitoes were more
active after sundown.

The German pastor and his wife came out to see them
off. Herr Schmitt had lived in Africa for most of his life,
and was by now incapable of imagining any other existence. Conversation between then had not been extensive,
owing to the problems of language, but over supper the
night before, they had been able to tell them that a man
called Alex Gantry had been living in Gstango. This
morning they had sent a message to the police at
Gstango, informing them of the enquiries which were
being made, and this afternoon, they had been informed,

transport would arrive to take Mrs Gantry and her escort to the small mining town fifteen miles north of Bakoua.

Remembering what Alex had said about Gstango being only fifty miles from the capital, Olivia couldn't help wondering where they had gone wrong. They must have covered well over a hundred miles in the past two days—or perhaps it only seemed that way!'

'Mrs Gantry?' The black driver of the jeep had mounted the shallow steps to the verandah and was now addressing himself to Olivia.

'Yes,' she nodded.

'Inspector Roche sent me to escort you to Gstango, Mrs Gantry. Sergeant Kasaba, at your service.'

'How do you do?' Olivia smiled, relieved to find that his English was almost perfect. 'Er—this is my—friend, Francis Kennedy. We're both ready to leave whenever you wish.'

Sergeant Kasaba inclined his head, and after exchanging a few words with the Schmitts, he carried their leather holdalls down to the jeep. They had left most of their belongings at the hotel in Ashenghi, being advised by the authorities there that they would find suitcases an encumbrance on their trip into the bush.

Francis offered to sit in the back of the jeep, but Olivia wouldn't hear of it. She insisted he took the sprung seat beside the driver, and she clambered into the back, along with a spade, several bamboo canes, twine, and a rifle.

It was almost dark by the time the lights of the settlement had disappeared behind them. The jeep pitched its way through rough jungle for some distance, before emerging into open savannah, and Olivia was soaked by the drops of moisture that fell from the trees they passed and plopped down on to her head and her bare forearms. At least, she hoped it was only rainwater, she thought uneasily. Who knew what manner of creature might hang in the trees waiting for an unwary traveller? The idea of snakes was about as attractive as that of the spiders earlier, and she hunched her shoulders up round her ears and maintained a stalwart silence.

'You have been long in my country, Mr Kennedy?' she heard Sergeant Kasaba asking Francis, but she hardly listened to their stilted exchange. She was too intent on the prospect of reaching their destination, and the eventual revelations it would entail.

It seemed hours before they reached Gstango, but Olivia had lost any real conception of time. Besides, there was something rather eerie about driving across Africa at night, with the unfamiliar sounds of the animals for company. She thought she heard lions at one point, and her heart almost stopped beating at the realisation of how little protection the jeep afforded. But more disturbing still was the unearthly cry of the hyena, that reminded Olivia of all the horror stories she had ever read.

They reached Gstango soon after seven o'clock. Olivia was amazed to find that contrary to her expectations, the small mining community had developed itself into quite a thriving little town. There were shops and prefabricated housing, and even a cinema, advertising an American film. There was a hospital—*of course*! That was where Lilian had worked. And a combined fire and police station, not far from the mine itself. The only thing it seemed to lack was an hotel, and Olivia's heart sank dejectedly at the prospect of maybe having to drive back to the Mission tonight.

'Inspector Roche will see you here,' announced their driver, drawing up outside the lighted windows of the police station. He climbed down and came round to help Olivia. 'If you will come this way.'

Francis was frankly swaying on his feet by this time,

and although Olivia ached from the jolting journey in the back of the jeep she was more concerned about him than herself.

'Would—would you rather stay here?' she ventured, touching his sleeve, but Francis shook his head.

'What—with all the mosquitoes?' he asked, trying to make light of his condition; and Olivia let him lean on her as they approached the building.

But there was another hitch. There had, explained an official, been a slight accident at the mine. Inspector Roche had been called away only minutes before. His suggestion was that Mrs Gantry and her friend should be shown to their accommodation, and the inspector would find time to speak to them in the morning.

Olivia's spirits swooped, but she saw that Francis was taking the news with infinite relief. Of course, she was being completely selfish, thinking of herself again, she thought, in sudden recrimination. After a night's sleep, Francis would, she hoped, feel better, and one day more or less was not going to make that much difference.

'Where are we to stay?' she asked, realising she ought to be grateful they were not being asked to return to Bakoua and come back again tomorrow. At least the good inspector had arranged for them to stay overnight, which was something in a community of this kind.

They were shown to bungalows, not far from the police station. Evidently they were normally used by members of the mining administration. They were single units, comprising living room, bedroom, kitchen and bathroom, and to Francis' evident disapproval, he was expected to occupy the one next door to Olivia's.

'I can sleep on the couch in the living room,' he exclaimed, although his appearance evidently belied such a claim.

'Don't be silly.' Olivia reassured him firmly, squeezing his arm through the damp cotton of his shirt. 'Honestly,

Francis, I'll be fine. And besides, the walls aren't so thick that I can't attract your attention, if I need to.'

Francis was not happy, but weakness and weariness were taking their toll. And besides, Sergeant Kasaba seemed totally bewildered by the Englishman's attitude, and Olivia guessed he could see no reason for Francis' concern.

'There is food in the refrigerator,' he indicated, as if this would appease Francis' objections. 'Or can I bring you something from the company canteen——'

'Oh, no!'

Francis turned even paler, and Olivia hastily rescued the situation. 'We're not hungry, thank you, Sergeant,' she assured him firmly. 'And as you say, if we are, we can help ourselves. Thank you for your hospitality— we're really very grateful.'

Sergeant Kasaba went away with a slightly more favourable attitude towards their uninvited visitors, and Olivia pushed Francis towards his own door.

'Go to bed,' she told him gently. 'I'll see you in the morning. Right now, I think all we both need is sleep.'

Nevertheless, despite what she had told Francis, Olivia was not entirely happy when she settled down for the night. It wasn't that she was nervous, exactly. It was just that it was all so strange, so different from what she had imagined; and she was a little apprehensive, too, of what Inspector Roche had to say to her.

She must have fallen asleep, however, because when she opened her eyes again it was with the distinct awareness of having been disturbed. Something, or someone, had awoken her, and her skin crawled uneasily with the knowledge of her isolation. Was Francis awake? Would he hear her if she called him? And how could she disturb him, when she didn't even know what had awakened her? It could have been the sound of a car outside; they were near enough the road. Or it could have been the siren from the mine. She had heard a wailing sound earlier. It could be any one of a hundred different sounds which had aroused her from her slumber, and the idea that it was something threatening was all inside her head.

Even so, she was intensely aware of her own vulnerability beneath the single sheet which was all that covered her. She was wearing no pyjamas or nightgown, nothing which might conceivably be described as night attire. She had slept naked since her arrival in Tsaba, and she had seen no reason to change her routine. She had showered earlier, beneath the tepid spray that issued from the tap in the bathroom, and she had felt delightfully cool when she climbed into bed. But she wasn't cool now. She was sweating. And her nerves tightened anxiously as she strained her ears for any sound.

The opening of her bedroom door was totally unexpected even so, as was the stream of light issuing through from the living room. It profiled the frame of the man who had opened the door, but cast his face into shadow, and an involuntary cry escaped her lips.

'What the hell——' The man groped impatiently for the light switch, and Olivia cowered beneath the sheet as lamplight flooded the room.

'Liv!'

'Alex!'

They both spoke simultaneously, but it was Alex who first recovered himself. 'Liv!' he muttered angrily. 'For God's sake, I thought you were still in Bakoua!'

Olivia clutched the sheet under her chin, her whole body quivering at the sight of the one man she had least expected to see. What was Alex doing here? How had he got here so quickly? And what was he doing in her bungalow, when she had imagined him thousands of miles away, with his family in England?

'I—why—why are you here, Alex?' she got out falteringly, as he thrust his hand inside his shirt and massaged the taut muscles of his chest.

'Why?' he snapped shortly. 'Surely you can guess why. I came after you, of course. As soon as I found out what harebrained scheme you had in mind.'

Olivia expelled her breath. 'There—there was no need. I don't need your assistance. Francis is with me——'

'So where is he?'

'Where is he?' Olivia gazed at him with shocked eyes. 'Why, next door, of course. Where did you think he would be? In here with me?'

'It would make more sense,' muttered Alex savagely, and Olivia's fears and resentment exploded in an angry retaliation.

'Don't judge everyone by your standards!' she retorted hotly, wishing she could get out of bed and confront him. He always put her at a disadvantage. He could stand there, arguing with her, arrogantly superior in his shirt and jeans, while she was forced to hide under the covers, like a frightened rabbit. 'And you still haven't explained what you're doing in here? Unless you hoped to expose our relationship!'

'Whose relationship?' he demanded, approaching the bed, viewing her with dark disturbing eyes.

'Why—why, mine and Francis', of course,' she declared tremulously. 'That is what you've insinuated, isn't it? That we're more than just friends?'

'And aren't you?'

'Of course not. Francis—Francis is a friend, a good friend. Something you seem to know nothing about.'

'Indeed?'

He towered over her, a terrifying threat to both her body and her senses, and she knew she had to keep talking or Armageddon might overtake her.

'I—I wish you would leave,' she said unsteadily. 'You have no right to be in here.'

'Wrong. This is my bungalow—or at least it was, before I went away.'

Olivia's lips parted. 'I—I don't believe you——'

'That's your prerogative.'

Olivia was thinking fast. Was he speaking the truth? Would Sergeant Kasaba—or Inspector Roche, for that matter—have put her in Alex Gantry's bungalow, probably believing she had come here on Alex's behalf? It was not as unreasonable as she had at first imagined.

'Then—I'm sorry,' she muttered unwillingly. 'I had no idea.'

'That I can believe.' Alex inclined his head. 'After what happened the other night, I'm sure you'd have taken anyone's bungalow but mine.'

Olivia hunched her shoulders. 'The other night—I was distraught——'

'And you're not now?'

'No.' Olivia moistened her lips. 'Alex, we can't talk now. I—Francis might overhear us——'

'That's unlikely.'

'Unlikely?'

'Sure. Hadn't you noticed? The bedrooms are situated on the outer walls of the bungalows.'

Olivia glanced round. He was right, but she had been too tired earlier to notice it. It was the kitchen and the bathroom that shared the party wall with the bungalow next door.

'Well—well, anyway,' she stammered, forcing back the sense of panic that was rising inside her, 'this—this is neither the time nor the place to conduct this kind of conversation. We can talk in the morning——'

'As we did in England?' he reminded her harshly.

'That—that was different. And besides, you weren't there.'

'And you left before I got back.'

'I shan't be leaving here,' she declared tautly. 'Not

until I know the truth.'

'Is that so?' His lips twisted wryly. 'Well, I can supply you with some facts you won't find in Gstango.'

Olivia moved her head uneasily. 'Not now, Alex——'

'Why not now? What are you afraid of?' He squatted down beside the bed, his expression ironic. 'Wouldn't you be relieved to know that we're not brother and sister?' he probed, stroking one brown finger along the taut line of the sheet she had clamped beneath her chin.

Olivia trembled. 'Please,' she breathed, 'go away, Alex. I don't want to scream, but I will if you don't get out of here.'

'What? And bring half the police force of Gstango in here?' he mocked, fingering the coil of dark hair that spilled carelessly over her shoulders. 'Oh, Liv, you wouldn't do that, would you?'

'Go away!' Olivia released one arm from the sheet to sweep the rope of her hair over the shoulder farthest from him. 'I don't know what you hope to gain, coming after me like this. Unless you're afraid of what I'm about to find out.'

'Afraid?' His night-dark eyes flashed dangerously. 'What would I have to be afraid of, Liv?'

'I don't know, do I?' Olivia's nerves were stretched almost to breaking point. 'That's what I'm here to find out. And—and if you were any kind of a man, you'd respect my right to do so. Instead of abandoning your—your real responsibilities!'

'And what are my real responsibilities?' he demanded softly, shifting sideways on to the edge of the bed. And while Olivia hurriedly moved her legs out of his way, he added. 'Aren't they to myself? To the things I want and need? To the pursuit of my own fulfilment?'

Olivia gasped. 'No! Not if they're at the expense of other people.'

'Other people?'

The mildness of his tone did not delude her into thinking he was prepared to listen to her, but she had to go on: 'Yes,' she said now. 'Your—your responsibilities should be towards—towards Lilian; and your son.' She hesitated only a moment before hastening on: 'You can't deny Sacha is Henry's grandson. The resemblance is too distinctive. Why—why, even Mrs Winters remarked upon it.'

'All right,' Alex's voice was hard now, 'so Sacha is Henry's grandson. Where does that leave us?'

'Us?' Olivia gazed at him helplessly, the confirmation he had given her tearing any tenuous hopes she had into shreds.

'Yes, us!' he repeated harshly, leaning towards her. 'Don't pretend this charade is solely for my benefit. You wanted to know what our relationship was before you committed yourself.'

'Committed myself?' Olivia's lips parted. 'To—to what?'

'To this,' he told her roughly, and grasping her trembling shoulders, he jerked her into his arms.

'No, Alex——' she choked against his lips, but the suffocating pressure of his mouth stifled her protest. He was grim and angry, and in consequence his kiss was not gentle at all, just a savage assault that she was incapable of preventing. With ruthless determination he forced her back against her pillows, and her muscles slackened beneath the muscled weight of his body.

Hot tears spilled helplessly from her eyes, running heedlessly down her cheeks. How could he? she asked herself bitterly. How could he take advantage of her like this, in full knowledge of his relationship with Lilian, and the son they shared? It was unforgivable!

'Oh, Liv,' he groaned suddenly, tasting the salty tang of her tears on his lips. 'Liv, don't cry! For God's sake, don't cry!' He released her mouth to seek the soft curve

of her throat, his tongue soft and sensual against her
skin. 'Lilian means nothing to me, I swear it. You're the
only woman I've ever truly wanted. That's why I came
after you. I couldn't stand to think of you and Kennedy,
alone together.'

'And—and do you think that's enough?' she gasped,
trying to push him away from her. 'You think because you—you say you want me, I should be—be flattered——'

'Don't talk rubbish, Liv,' he muttered, and overcom-
ing her protesting fingers, he pulled the sheet away from
her shoulders.

The swollen arousal of her breasts was unmistakable,
and although she tried to press his head away, the
kindling passion of his gaze was igniting a flame inside
her. When he tore the buttons of his shirt apart and
brought her resisting hands to his chest, her fingers
curled convulsively against him. The rough whorls of
sun-streaked body hair that clung to her skin were
seductively warm and sensual, and when his lips
captured the taut peak of one rounded breast a sharp
pain flowered deep inside her.

'Liv—*Liv*!' he breathed, dragging the rest of the covers
aside to expose the slender nakedness of her body. 'Oh,
Liv—don't fight me, please!'

'Alex——'

'I want you, Liv,' he said, against her mouth, opening
her lips to his. 'Let me—let me love you——'

Olivia felt a wave of weakness sweeping over her. He
was so disturbingly male, so persuasive; and if this
aching void she felt inside her was to be assuaged only
he could do it. With a little sob, she submitted to the
searching heat of his mouth, drugged by the emotions
his caressing hands were arousing, and responding instinctively to the demands her flesh was making.

She was hardly aware of him shedding the rest of his

clothes, until she felt the hard warmth of him beside her. The strong muscles of his chest crushed her softness, pressing her down into the soft mattress, and one lithe powerful leg nudged her legs apart.

'No, Alex——' she whispered one last time, as the realisation of what she was doing caused a momentary withdrawal, but it was only a perfunctory denial. With her arms wound silkily around his neck, and her nails dug deep into the hair at his nape, she could not have let him go, and Alex was swiftly driven beyond any needs but his own.

He covered her lips and her cheeks and her eyes with urgent hungry kisses that left her breathless, and weak with longing, and innocence gave way to passion as she arched her body into his. Twisting beneath him, feeling the pulsating heat that throbbed against her, she still had no real idea of what she was inviting. She only knew she wanted him to go on and on, until whatever it was that was driving her was satisfied . . .

It was the light that disturbed her, the awareness of brightness bearing down on her lids that caused her to open her eyes in protest. For a fraction of a second, a sense of disorientation gripped her, but as the austere surroundings of the bungalow bedroom swung back into focus, she met Alex's dark eyes and knew what she had done.

Even then, she did not immediately move to cover herself. She lay, staring into that narrowed slumbrous gaze with unknowing adoration, unable in those first few moments to disguise the rapturous abandon that still gripped her.

It was Alex who moved, Alex who tossed the crumpled sheet across the lissom invitation of her body; Alex, who was already dressed and looking now as if he despised her as well as himself.

'Why didn't you tell me?' he snapped, pacing violently about the room. 'For God's sake, Liv, why didn't you tell me? Surely you knew I would never have touched you!'

Olivia shivered then, as the cool wind of disillusionment brushed her scorched flesh. He had taken her, believing her to be as experienced as he evidently was. By the time he had discovered the truth, it had been too late to draw back.

Wrapping the sheet about her, she looked at him with wounded eyes. 'What's wrong?' she demanded, forcing back a humiliating sense of inadequacy. 'Didn't you enjoy it? Didn't I do it right? I'm sorry, I didn't know I was supposed to produce references——'

'Stop it!' Alex cut her off abruptly, his lean face taut with anger. 'You know damn well what I'm talking about. And it has nothing to do with whether or not we— made it good!'

Olivia lifted her shoulders. 'I thought it did.'

'*Liv!*' He stopped beside her, looking down at her with tormented eyes. Then, shaking his head, he said wearily: 'You know how it was—for me, at least.' He paused. 'Did I hurt you a lot?'

Olivia trembled. 'Does it matter?' In truth, the pain she had experienced had been swiftly superseded by the mounting wave of fulfilment Alex had created. The urgent power of his body in hers had been the most wonderful experience of her whole life, but how could she tell him that when he obviously regretted the whole affair?

'Hell, Liv,' he said now, pushing back the damp strands of sun-streaked hair that had strayed across his forehead, 'I never dreamt the old man might not have touched you!' He smote the palm of one hand against his temple. 'He really must have cared about you, after all.'

'No!' Olivia could not take that, not from him! With a jack-knifing movement she left the bed, wrapping the sheet sarong-wise about her. 'He didn't care-about me. But once, I think, he cared about my mother.' She moved impatiently. 'I've told you how it was. What I didn't tell you was that your father ruined my father. He destroyed him, just as surely as if he'd taken a knife and killed him. That was why I agreed to marry Henry Gantry—because my mother wanted her revenge.' She shook her head. 'There was no question of my being his daughter. I think—I think you've just made that up.'

'No.' Alex shook his head now, sliding his hands into the hip pockets of his jeans, parting his unbuttoned shirt and making Olivia unwillingly aware even after what had happened, she was still not immune to his dangerous attraction. 'It wasn't that simple, Liv. Ask Cosgrove when we get back to England, if you don't believe me. How did Henry come to contact your mother, only weeks before he died, if it wasn't a carefully planned operation?'

Olivia gasped. 'Henry—Henry knew he was dying. When he was told he had only a short time to live, he came to find my mother. He wanted *her* to marry him. He wanted to make amends for what had happened— or so he said.'

'No.' Alex shook his head again, and she stared at him white-faced. 'No, it wasn't like that, Liv. Could you honestly see a man like Henry Gantry regretting anything? When he could cut his only son off without a penny!'

Olivia swallowed. She had never thought of it in that light. But if Henry had not felt remorse, what had he felt?

'I think you'd better sit down,' said Alex now, but when he would have guided her to a chair, she flinched away from him, and his face darkened angrily. 'I'm only telling you this to prepare you,' he muttered, clenching his fists. 'And to try and justify what I believed.'

Olivia held up her head. 'Just tell me what you have to say. Don't try to excuse yourself. I—I'll never forgive you for what you've done, so you might as well get to the point.'

Alex looked grim, but common sense—or his conscience—forced him to proceed, and with harsh inflection, he said: 'It was your mother who contacted Henry.' And at Olivia's cry of denial, he went on: 'When she read about Henry Gantry's illness in a newspaper, she devised a scheme to defraud him of at least a percentage of his fortune——'

'No!'

'Yes.' Alex was adamant. 'I can prove it, should that be necessary. For the moment, you'll have to take my word for it.' He paused, momentarily drawn by her shocked face, and then continued: 'She contacted Henry, I know this for a fact, and she succeeded in persuading him that he had a daughter, as well as a son.'

'I don't believe this!'

'No. Nor did Henry, I suspect, at first. But have you ever compared the date of your birth with your mother's affair with Henry Gantry?'

Olivia made a gesture of negation.

'So . . .' Alex moved his shoulders. 'They match. Indeed they do. You could conceivably have been Henry's daughter.'

'No!' But Olivia's cry was feeble now.

'Henry had doubts, serious doubts, but can you imagine how it was with him at that time? He was dying. He knew he had only a short time to live. And in addition to which, after meeting you, he was flattered enough not to want to enquire too closely.'

'I don't believe you!'

Alex sighed. 'Think about it. Paternity is always difficult to prove. And besides, he saw you as the means of disinheriting his son.'

'So that's why you came back!'

Alex inclined his head. 'As it was, he knew he hadn't the time to prove or disprove your identity. And in any case, he knew that a daughter's claim was very small change to that of a wife. So he married you, and your mother consented—knowing full well you were *not* Henry Gantry's daughter!'

Olivia wet her dry lips. 'I—I'm not?'

'Fortunately, in this day and age, even if paternity cannot always be proved, it can be disproved. According to the medical you had at the time of your marriage, your blood group matches neither Henry Gantry's nor your mother's.'

Olivia digested this. She remembered having the medical very well, and wondering why Henry had instigated it. She had assumed his own ill health had made him overly concerned for the health of others.

'Then—then Henry must have known——'

'Not necessarily. Your mother's medical records were not freely available until after her death. And besides, as I said, Henry wanted to believe it.'

'And—and you're saying—Adam Cosgrove knew?'

'He was Henry's solicitor. He knew everything that happened.'

Olivia felt hopelessly confused, and hopelessly defeated. She had come here, to find out the truth about Alex's identity, and instead she had lost her own. In retrospect, what Alex had told her was not so hard to believe. Her mother's lack of surprise at Henry's sudden appearance after more than twenty years; her insistence that Olivia should do as he said, when she had known he was not a man to be trusted. At the time, Olivia had put it down to her mother's illness. And besides, she had had her own reasons for wanting to hurt Henry

Gantry. But suddenly everything was changed, and the ambiguity of her position had never been more obvious.

As if taking pity on her, Alex came towards her, but now Olivia held him off with a hastily-raised arm. 'Don't—don't come near me,' she whispered shakily. 'I—I have to think about this. I—I have to decide what I must do.'

'I have to tell you, I've only found these things out in the last few days,' Alex offered flatly. 'That was why I was so bitter in the beginning. I really believed you'd taken the old man for everything he had.'

'Is—is that supposed to be an apology?' Olivia was contemptuous.

'No.' Alex's hard face was grave. 'I'm just saying—we were both victims of our own misapprehensions.' He hesitated. 'I didn't know I was going to fall in love with you.'

Olivia swayed. 'You can't be serious!'

'After what's happened?' He spread his hands. 'I don't blame you for not believing me. But I knew this might be the only chance I'd get, and I wanted you.'

Olivia turned away, appalled by his confession. He was Henry's son! Had he no shame?

'I think you'd better leave,' she said huskily, bending her head, and Alex made a sound of assent. But the imprint of his lips lingered on her shoulder, after the door had closed behind him.

CHAPTER TEN

In the pale light of morning, Gstango looked like any other mining community. It was primarily a functional base for mining personnel, its amenities catering for the needs of men temporarily cut off from their families.

From the balcony of her bungalow, Olivia could see the main road into the settlement, which she and Francis had travelled the night before, and the huddle of community and administration buildings, where Inspector Roche had his office.

The mine itself was visible in the distance, the clouds of dust rising from its bulldozers in direct contrast to the damp earth around the bungalow. It must have rained in the night, but she had not heard it. After Alex had left her, she had fallen into a deep dreamless sleep, which had left her this morning feeling decidedly hungover.

She had no idea where Alex had gone after he left the bungalow. At first, she had been half afraid he might have bedded down on the couch in the living room as Francis had suggested doing, but this morning's tentative foray had quickly relieved her of that belief, although not knowing where he was was almost as disturbing.

She wondered if there was any point in speaking to Inspector Roche, after what Alex had told her. It seemed obvious that she had been the victim of both her mother's and Henry's ambitions, and it was hard to be objective, when the facts as she had known them no longer applied. All that was real was that she had lived a lie for the past six or seven months. She had been used by two unscrupulous people to gain their own ends, and she had been too stupid to see it for herself.

Francis appeared as she was brushing her hair, and she welcomed him eagerly, glad to see a friendly face. He looked bleary-eyed and pale-faced, but evidently less feverish than the day before, and Olivia urged him into a chair before he had chance to ask any questions. But apparently Francis knew nothing of Alex's arrival, and his first words to her were not complimentary.

'You don't look as if you slept at all,' he remarked, heaving a sigh. 'Will I be glad to get back to civilisation! Living life in the rough is certainly not for us.'

Olivia forced a smile. 'Actually—actually, I slept rather well,' she averred, turning away, ostensibly to secure the leather cord at her nape. 'How—how about you? You weren't disturbed, were you?'

'Disturbed?' Francis arched his brows. 'By what?' His eyes narrowed. 'You didn't have an intruder!'

'No. At least——' Olivia moved her shoulders awkwardly, 'Alex—Alex is here. In Gstango. He—he came to the bungalow, after—after you'd gone to bed.'

She omitted to say that it was after she had gone to bed, too, but Francis was not concerned with the technicalities. 'Gantry!' he exclaimed. 'Alex Gantry is here? I don't believe it. How could he be? We've only just arrived here ourselves.'

'Well, he is,' Olivia assured him firmly, keeping the tremor out of her voice by a supreme effort of will power. 'Believe me, I was as shocked as you are. I—he says he was—concerned about—about us.'

Francis snorted. 'Concerned about what we'd find out about him,' he declared shortly. 'Hell, he really is the limit. Particularly after what you told me about his wife and son!'

'She's not his wife,' Olivia corrected, but Francis was not really listening to her. Ever since she had felt bound to tell him about Alex bringing Lilian Eve and her baby to stay at the house, Francis had been disapproving, and this present development was evidently as unpalatable.

'I can't understand why Cosgrove puts his trust in him!' he exclaimed now. 'I mean—Alex Gantry was never the saint you seem to think him. Oh, he had a hard time of it all right, when his mother died. But afterwards, long before he knew the truth about her death, he was a source of great distress to his father.'

Olivia turned to him now. 'How?'

'Oh, the usual way.' Francis sighed. 'There were always girls—from the minute he was old enough to know the difference. Girls, and when he was old enough, motorbikes and fast cars. His father bought him out of a dozen different scrapes before Alex delivered the final insult.'

Olivia shook her head. 'I didn't know that.'

'Well, you wouldn't, would you? I doubt Alex would betray that kind of confidence. Besides, he probably believes the world owes him, instead of the other way around.'

'Yes.' But Olivia was disturbed, and she was glad when they were interrupted by the arrival of a man in white overalls, carrying a tray. The smell of hot rolls and coffee was tantalising, and the man's black face creased into a wide smile as he set the tray on the table.

' 'spector Roche thought you'd like some breakfast,' he drawled, straightening. 'He says he'll see you in thirty minutes, if you'll come down to the office.'

'Thank you.' Olivia was grateful.

'A pleasure, ma'am,' the man essayed politely, and let himself out again as she turned to the tray.

'Hmm, hot rolls,' she breathed, inviting Francis to join her as she spread one liberally with butter from an iced container. 'I'd forgotten how hungry I was.'

This time Inspector Roche was waiting for them when they entered the administration building. He turned out to be a tall fair-skinned South African, and his smile was friendly as he invited them into his office.

'Mrs Gantry,' he greeted her smoothly, urging her to a chair. 'And Mr—Kennedy? Am I right? Mr Graham was here earlier, and he told me your name.'

Olivia blinked. Who was Mr Graham? But this was no time to concern herself with trivialities, and linking her hands in her lap, she said: 'You know why we've come?'

Inspector Roche picked up a pack of cigarettes from his desk, and after offering it to both of them and being refused, he put a long slim cylinder between his lips. 'There was a man in Ashenghi recently who claimed to be a representative of the—Gantry corporation, am I right?'

Francis nodded. 'That would be Philip Ndobe.'

'Ndobe? Yes, I believe you're right.' Roche flicked his lighter and lit his cigarette. 'But I didn't know this man, and I'd had no instructions from Mr Graham to give him the information he wanted.'

Olivia sighed. 'Well, that's not important now, is it? We're here. And we are bona fide representatives of the company. I—my husband was Henry Gantry. Alex Gantry's father.'

'Yes. Yes, I know.' Roche inclined his head, and Olivia wondered rather irritably whether 'Mr Graham' had told him that too. 'And you want to know what happened to Mr Gantry—Mr Alex Gantry, that is. For some pecuniary reasons pertaining to his late father's estate.'

'You could put it like that.' Francis exchanged a wry look with Olivia. 'First of all, would you recognise Alex Gantry if you saw him?'

Roche stared at him in evident bewilderment. 'I beg your pardon?'

Francis made an impatient gesture. 'Alex Gantry—do you know Alex Gantry?'

'I did.'

'So you'd recognise him if you saw him?'

'I would,' Roche nodded. But before Olivia could draw an uneven breath, he added: 'However, as Alex Gantry is dead, I don't——'

Olivia came round to find herself lying on a couch in Inspector Roche's office. She had not noticed the couch earlier, or the fly-spotted ceiling; but now she had plenty of time to observe both as Francis sat beside her, patting her hand.

'Olivia!' he was saying agitatedly. 'Oh, Olivia, please wake up!'

'Would you get out of my way?' Inspector Roche shifted Francis aside and bent over Olivia capably, offering a cup of cool water to her parched lips. 'Drink this,' he urged, cradling her against his shoulder. 'It's the heat. You're probably a little dehydrated.'

Olivia sipped the water gratefully, but as her memory returned to her, she knew it was not the heat that had made her lose consciousness. It was the news that Alex Gantry was dead. *Dead!* Which meant that the man masquerading as him was an impostor.

By the time she had finished the glass of water, Olivia was feeling well enough to sit up, and Inspector Roche resumed his seat. 'Shall we go on?' he suggested, glancing at Francis, and Olivia nodded before he could respond.

'Please,' she said, holding herself stiffly. 'You—you were saying Alex Gantry was dead. Can—can you tell us how that happened?'

'Of course.' Roche riffled through some papers on his desk and produced a narrow file. 'This contains a copy of the report the South African authorities prepared at the time of his death——'

'The *South African* authorities!' Olivia was blank.

'Yes.' Roche sighed. 'You didn't know he was living in South Africa at the time of his death?'

'No.' Olivia shook her head. 'I understood——' She gestured towards the windows. 'The mine . . .'

'Ah.' Roche nodded. 'You knew he was one of the original owners of Gstango Ore?'

'Original?' Olivia was confused.

'Of course. Gantry abandoned the scheme years ago. I'm afraid your stepson was not interested in the long-term benefits of the development. The mine was going through a bad patch. Money was scarce. Gantry cut his losses, and sold out.'

'I see.' Olivia put an unsteady hand to her head. 'And—and Alex's partner?'

'Mr Graham?' So that was who Mr Graham was! 'He managed to keep the mine going. It was tough, but he made it, and since we discovered this area is rich in pitchblende——'

'Pitchblende!' Francis interrupted him now, and Olivia gazed at him in surprise.

'Yes, pitchblende,' agreed Roche dryly. 'I see you are not unfamiliar with its by-products, Mr Kennedy. Gstango Ore has become one of the most profitable developments in the world.'

Olivia shook her head. 'I'm afraid I——'

'Uranium, Mrs Gantry,' Roche inserted smoothly. 'The Tsaban government has granted the sole concession to Gstango Ore.'

She tried to take it in. 'So—Alex would have been rich, had he lived.'

'No.' Francis was impatient. 'I told you, Mrs Gantry, Alex was a loser. He sold out. Inspector Roche has just said so.'

'That's true,' Roche nodded. 'But I must tell you, Mr Graham had tried to find him. Unfortunately, by the time he was successful Alex Gantry was dead.'

'When did Alex leave? When did he go away?'

Roche frowned. 'A little over two years ago.' He sighed. 'There were other—problems, of a personal nature. I don't think I should go into them.'

'Oh, please.' Olivia was urgent. 'I—I wish you would. What kind of personal problems?'

Roche hesitated. 'It concerns a young woman——'

'Lilian Eve!'

'How did you know?'

'Does it matter?' Olivia shook her head. 'Go on.'

'Well,' Roche moved his shoulders, 'she's a fellow countrywoman of mine—a nurse, at the hospital here in Gstango. She—she became involved with Alex Gantry. I think she thought he might marry her. In any event, he didn't, and soon after he went away she found she was pregnant.'

Olivia shivered. 'It was—Alex's child?'

'Without doubt.'

'Did he—did he know?'

'That I can't say.' Roche looked a little discomfited now. 'What is relevant is that she stayed on here, at Gstango, and had her baby.'

'A boy.'

'Yes.' Roche made no further reference to her fore-knowledge. 'When we discovered that Gantry was dead, Mr Graham made himself responsible for her. He wanted to give her a share of the mine, but she refused.'

Olivia caught her breath. 'This—this man—this Mr Graham you speak of, what—what does he look like?'

'Olivia!' Francis spoke involuntarily, her name spilling naturally from his lips.

'Wait, Francis,' she said, squeezing her hands tightly together. 'Well, Inspector? Does—does Mr Graham bear any resemblance to—to the man you knew as Alex Gantry?'

Roche frowned. 'Why do you want to know?'

'Please—just answer my question.'

Roche shrugged. 'Well, I suppose there were similarities. They were of a similar height and build.'

'And colouring?'

'Yes. Now you come to mention it, they were both fair-haired, although Mr Graham has much darker skin.'

'Thank you.' Olivia exchanged another charged look with Francis. 'I—I should like to speak to—to Mr Graham. Is that possible?'

'I'm afraid not.' Roche shook his head.

'You're afraid not!' Olivia got agitatedly to her feet. 'But you said—you said you'd spoken to him earlier.'

'I did. But he left soon after. He flew back to Ashenghi.' He paused. 'The head office of the mining company is there. But I believe he said he was flying back to England tonight.'

'Back—to England,' echoed Olivia faintly.

'Yes. He has—friends there. Why? I'm afraid I don't know their address, so I couldn't put you in contact with him.'

'That's all right.' Francis had got to his feet now, and it was he who answered the inspector. 'We—er—I think we've learned all we need to for the present.'

'I'm extremely sorry about your stepson, Mrs Gantry,' Roche offered, getting up also and holding out his hand in farewell. 'If you'd like to take the report, I have instructions that it may be offered to you.'

'Thank you.' Olivia accepted the folder. 'It was very good of you to see me.'

'Not at all.' Roche smiled, which took years off his somewhat tough appearance. 'By the way, Mr Graham has offered you the use of one of the company helicopters, should you prefer to fly back to Ashenghi.'

'A helicopter!' So that explained how Alex—*no, not*

Alex, Mr Graham, she corrected herself incredulously—
had been able to reach Gstango so quickly.

'We'd be very grateful.' Francis answered for both of
them, and Olivia could see how relieved he was at the
realisation they would not have to make the journey
overland again.

'Very well.' Roche showed them to the door. 'I will
contact the mine manager and let you know when
transport will be available. Until then, I suggest you
avail yourselves of the bungalows you occupied last
night. Goodbye.'

In Olivia's bungalow, Francis flung himself on to the
couch with a grunt of disbelief. 'Imagine it,' he said,
before she could make any comment. 'Alex Gantry is
really this Mr Graham! He has to be. But why is he
doing it, that's what I'd like to know!'

'For Sacha,' said Olivia at once, almost without conscious thought. 'Sacha is Henry's grandchild. And if he
hadn't been prepared to do something, nobody would.'

Olivia and Francis arrived back in London the following
evening. They were both exhausted, and after the brief-
est of farewells, Olivia went to find a taxi to take her
back to Chalcott. Francis had his own car at the airport,
but she refused to allow him to drive her home.

'We'll talk tomorrow,' she assured him firmly. 'And
thanks, Francis. Thanks for everything.'

The taxi ranks were busy, and she was leaning wearily
against a pillar when a hand touched her sleeve. 'Taxi,
lady?' an unmistakable voice offered softly, and she
swung round disbelievingly to find Alex standing behind
her.

'Alex!' she exclaimed, but he shook his head apologetically.

'_Leon_,' he corrected her dryly, picking up her belongings. 'Leon Graham. Come on—the car's over there. I

got held up in the traffic, and I thought for a minute I'd missed you.'

Olivia shook her head. 'It's so busy! I thought I was going to have to wait hours.'

'After waiting hours in Ashenghi, I know,' remarked Leon swinging open the Maserati's door. 'Get in. I'll dispose of these.'

Trying to disguise the way her hands were trembling, Olivia got into the front of the car, schooling her features to composure when he got in beside her.

'How—how did you get back to London before we did?' she ventured, as he negotiated the way out of the terminal area. 'I thought there only was one flight a day to England.'

'There is.' Leon accelerated into the tunnel. 'I took one of the mining company's flights to Lagos and got a connection from there.'

'I see,' Olivia nodded. She had expected to meet up with him in Ashenghi, but had been somewhat relieved to find he had already left. Somehow, the idea of meeting him again in Francis' company had not been appealing, particularly when her late husband's assistant was still suspicious of his motives.

They cleared the airport concourse, and once they were on the M4 heading for Maidenhead, he glanced her way. 'Well?' he said. 'Do you forgive me? Or am I forever damned for making such a mess of things?'

Olivia's tongue circled her lips. 'I think you'd better tell me about it. Then—then I can decide. Inspector Roche explained about Alex. I—I have his report in my bag.'

Leon added. 'Then you'll know how he died.'

'In a brawl in Johannesburg? Yes, I know. What I can't understand is, what was he doing there? And why did he leave Gstango, when there was every reason he should stay?'

Leon sighed. 'Let me tell you about Alex, hmm? Let me try and explain the kind of man he was.' He paused. 'I'm not saying he was a saint, but he wasn't as bad as that report seems to suggest.'

'Francis said he was a loser.'

'Yes. Yes, Francis would. And I guess he was, in a way. But that's the way somemen are made. They seem bent on a course of self-destruction. Alex was like that.'

Olivia tilted her head to one side. 'You liked him, didn't you? You really liked him.'

Leon acknowledged this with a faint inclination of his head. 'Yes. Yes, I liked him. When we met in 1971, I guess you could say we identified with one another.'

'You mean, you and your father quarrelled?'

'In a manner of speaking. Unfortunately, my father died before I could make amends. He never forgave me for abandoning a university career.'

'I see.'

'But that isn't relevant here, is it?' Leon grimaced. 'We're talking about Alex, about Alex's hang-ups, and I guess he was a bit of a tearaway.' He looked her way. 'How did you feel about him?'

'Latterly?' Olivia bent her head. 'I think you know the answer to that.'

Leon's hand pressed her knee for a moment, and then, doggedly, he went on: 'As I say, when Alex and I got together we had similar aims. We both wanted to succeed, for different reasons. The engineering job I'd gone out to Zambia to accept had fallen through, and I guess Alex had been mooching around for longer than that. Anyway, we got on together, and we told one another our troubles. I heard all about Chalcott, and the house and Alex's life there; and naturally I took Alex's part when it came to the matter of his father. We talked for hours and hours. I guess I got to know Chalcott as well as anyone can, who'd never been there.'

Olivia looked at him. 'Go on.'

'Well, we worked at various jobs, technical drawing, engineering, we even worked in a steel mill, but eventually we saved enough money to buy a concession at Gstango, and I guess Roche told you the rest.'

'He told us the mine had floundered for a while.'

'It did.' Leon pulled a wry face. 'As I said to you that first morning we talked together, quarrying minerals can be a soul-destroying business.'

'He—he also told us about—about Lilian.'

'Did he?' Leon frowned. 'Well, I guess it was relevant. That was how we found out what happened to Alex.'

'So he said.'

'Yes.' Leon hesitated. 'I suppose I should tell you how that happened——'

'You don't have to——'

'I do.' Leon was adamant. 'Let me see—I suppose it began as soon as Lilian came to Gstango. Even in a place as remote as that, we needed hospital facilities—men could be hurt, there were rock falls. Anyway, we eventually built up a small hospital staff, and among them, as you know, was Lilian.'

'Did Alex love her?'

'Love?' Leon grimaced. 'That's a strange word to use in connection with Alex. I don't know that he ever loved anyone, except perhaps his mother. After she died . . .' He shrugged.

'But he must have cared about her.'

'I suppose he thought as much of her as he was capable of feeling,' agreed Leon quietly. 'But it was never a tranquil relationship. Alex was too quick-tempered, too volatile; and when Lilian told him she was pregnant, he just took off without a second thought.'

'He took off?'

'Oh, the mine was having a bad time. Nobody wanted

our ore. The world was in recession, and it seemed likely we were going to fold.'

'But you didn't.'

'No, we didn't. We discovered uranium, in sufficient quantities to ensure the mine's survival.'

Olivia shook her head. 'Poor Alex!'

Leon sighed. 'How do you think I felt? Lilian had had the baby by then, and I wanted her to have what was rightfully hers. But she wouldn't listen. That was when I instituted enquiries to find Alex.'

'And—and Adam?'

'Cosgrove?' Leon shrugged. 'Well, he had kept in touch with Alex, as you know. When Alex disappeared, I wrote and informed him, and after that, he kept in touch with me.'

Olivia's lips parted. 'So—so Adam knew all along——'

'—that I wasn't Alex Gantry? Right.'

'That was why he tried to persuade me to wait before—before making any decision.'

'About appointing me chairman?' asked Leon wryly. 'Yes, he told me about that. I felt pretty sick, believe me.'

'But why?'

'Oh, Liv—when I came to England, I had some crazy idea of forcing you to acknowledge Sacha as Henry's grandchild. I hadn't the first idea how I was going to achieve that, so I improvised, all along the line. Oh, I admit, I did intend that you should think I was Alex, at least to begin with. I knew our appearance was sufficiently similar for it not to arouse any immediate suspicion, and pretending to be Alex enabled me to ask questions I couldn't have done as Leon Graham. Once I was installed in the house, it seemed a simple matter to introduce Lilian—and Sacha.'

'But how did you get in?'

'When Alex's effects were returned from Johannesburg, his keys were amongst them, and his passport. It wasn't too difficult to be accepted as Alex Gantry, particularly if one appeared confident.'

'You were certainly that,' commented Olivia wryly, and he smiled.

'Believe me, I was shaking in my shoes! But you made it so easy. You said—Alex? And I knew you believed I was who you said I was. If someone believes something, you're halfway there.'

Olivia sighed. 'I can hardly believe this.'

'Why? Because you want to—or you don't want to?'

Olivia's cheeks flamed in the darkness. 'Because I want to,' she said simply. 'Oh, Alex—Leon! whatever your name is—I'm so glad we're not related.'

'Yes. Yes, so am I,' said Leon quietly, and Olivia's palms moistened in anticipation of what this meant.

But to her dismay, he said nothing more. Instead, he went on to tell her that Alex's uncle had been a reluctant party to the deception, and that Sean had given him the information pertaining to her mother's involvement with Alex's father.

'It seems he was suspicious at the time,' he explained, while Olivia forced herself to concentrate on what he was saying. 'But it was Cosgrove who told me of Henry's doubts about your parentage, and gave me the lever I needed.'

Olivia fidgeted with her safety belt. 'I thought you hated me, you know,' she said, hoping to inspire some expression of affection, but Leon only shook his head.

'I did,' he admitted. 'Until I got to know you. Then I had the hardest time of all, trying to hold on to my original intentions.'

'You did?'

Once again Olivia waited for him to go on, but they were already running through the outskirts of Chalcott, and he said little more before they turned into Virginia Drive.

Mrs Winters was waiting on the steps for them. She had evidently heard the car, and she opened Olivia's door before Leon could walk round and do it for her.

'Mrs Gantry!' she exclaimed, with some concern, as Olivia got out of the car. 'My dear, you look worn out! Come along inside. I've got a nice supper waiting for you.'

Olivia wanted to protest that food was the last thing she needed, but she held her tongue as Mrs Winters had evidently gone to a lot of trouble. But the flight back from Tsaba had been frequently punctuated by the serving of meals, and in any case, her appetite had dwindled in the last few minutes.

They ate in the dining room, served by Mrs Winters herself, and the housekeeper's presence precluded any private conversation. She was too eager to impart the news of Sacha's latest antics, and it was obvious from her behaviour that she still had not learned the truth. Not that Olivia thought that would present any problems. She might be a little hurt at the deliberate deception, but when she learned why Leon had done it, she could not fail to feel admiration.

When the meal was over, Olivia excused herself to go to her room, but although Leon stood as a mark of politeness as she departed, he evidently had no intention of following her. On the contrary, now that he was back at the house he seemed brooding and morose, and the weariness that etched his features was as pronounced as her own.

A bath worked wonders, however, and by the time Mary had appeared and expressed her curiosity over her mistress's unexpected trip, Olivia felt wide awake again. She had put the girl off with some story about accompanying Francis on a business trip, and although

Mary seemed a little sceptical, she had been forced to accept it. But when the girl had left her, Olivia viewed her reflection rather wretchedly, realising as she did so that her story had not been so far from the truth. For some reason, Leon had chosen not to pursue his reasons for following her, and she wondered with a pang, whether he regretted making that confession. Perhaps it had been said in the heat of the moment; perhaps it had not really been true. Whatever the truth, she had to accept it, and wait for him to make the next move.

By two o'clock in the morning, Olivia was desperate. Sleep had eluded her, not a pleasant thing when she was as exhausted as her body had to be after more than twenty-four hours without rest. But her brain simply would not allow her to relax, and she decided to go down to the kitchen and make herself a warm drink.

Pulling a silk robe over the matching cream silk of her nightgown, she opened her bedroom door and trod softly along the corridor. The house was dark, but she was not afraid. With her thoughts for company, she did not even feel alone.

Nevertheless, she did give a start when another door opened farther along the corridor, and she fell back in surprise when Leon's tall figure appeared. Unlike her, he was still dressed, and she hung back in the shadows, praying he would not notice her. Where was he going? she wondered anxiously, half afraid even now he might have been lying, and that he and Lilian were more than just friends. But Leon moved in the direction of the stairs, and she tiptoed after him, holding her breath.

It was the leg of a console table that did it. As Leon was about to start downstairs Olivia, keeping out of sight, stubbed her toe on the leg of the table, and her sob of protest was blatantly audible.

'What the hell——'

Leon swung round and saw her at once, her cream robe visible even in the shadows. 'Liv!' he muttered impatiently, coming back along the corridor to where she was standing, rubbing her toe against her other foot. 'What on earth are you doing at this time of night?'

'I—I couldn't sleep.' Olivia looked up at him anxiously, her face pale in the dim light. 'When—when I saw you, I didn't want you to think I was following you.'

'But you were?'

'Only indirectly. I—I was going to go down to the kitchen to get a drink.'

'Isn't it a little late to be wanting a drink?'

'I thought it might help me to sleep,' she explained, intensely conscious of him, of his nearness, of the knowledge of the night they had spent together. 'Oh— Leon!' Her control snapped abruptly. 'Didn't you mean what you said when you said you loved me?'

Leon's face darkened, and then, with an abrupt movement, he took hold of her arm and urged her across the corridor and into the suite of rooms he had occupied since he came to Chalcott.

'Love you?' he grated, as the door closed behind them, and they were alone in the lamplighted room. 'Of course I love you! But you know as well as I do that Henry Gantry's widow is far beyond my reach!'

Olivia's lips parted, and as if he couldn't bear to be near her without touching her, he put the space of the room between them. Then, raking back his hair with an unsteady hand, he said savagely:

'Look, I guess this is all my fault. I—I should never have followed you out to Gstango. And I certainly should never have—taken advantage of you as I did. You said you'd never forgive me——'

'But that was *before*!' Olivia's voice was imploring. 'Leon, that was before I knew who you were. I—I thought you were Alex. Don't you see?'

'Okay.' He expelled his breath wearily. 'Okay, I'll accept that we both spoke in the heat of the moment——'

'Is that all it was?' Olivia took a few uncertain steps towards him. 'Leon, I—I don't believe you. I *can't* believe you. And please, stop behaving as if I was some kind of leper!'

'Leper!' Leon groaned. 'Oh, Liv, I'm the leper, can't you see that?'

'Why? Because you made love to me?' Olivia was rapidly decreasing the space between them. 'Leon, I wanted you to do it. I—I've not exactly kept you at arm's length, have I?'

'If only it were that simple,' he muttered, turning away.

'It is that simple,' Olivia insisted, reaching him and impulsively sliding her arms around his waist from behind. 'Oh, Leon,' she breathed, pressing her face against the thin cotton of his shirt, pressing herself against him. 'Leon, I love you. Isn't that enough?'

She could feel his body trembling, but still he didn't turn, and only when her fingers slid lower, over the flatness of his stomach, did his hands move to still hers.

'Liv!' he groaned. 'Oh, Liv, don't do this!'

'Why not?' Her voice was breathy, but it had gained a little confidence from his evident reaction. 'Leon, I want you to love me. Then we might both get some rest.'

Leon turned then, twisting round in her arms and putting his hands hard on her shoulders, propelling her way from him. 'It can't be,' he muttered. 'Liv, it can't be! Okay, call it stupid, if you like, but I refuse to marry a woman who can buy and sell me a dozen times over!'

Olivia's eyes widened. 'What do you mean?'

'Liv, Adam told me how it is. You might be only the

custodian of Henry's affairs, but you're still a wealthy woman for all that. God, if you gave half of what you had to Sacha, you'd still be a millionairess several times over. I—I can't take that. And I couldn't ask you to give it all up.' He sighed. 'I'm a miner, Liv. Oh, okay, Gstango Ore is making great strides, and I don't have to live on the site like I used to. But I do have to live in Tsaba. My home is there. And you couldn't commute, because I wouldn't let you.'

'But I don't have to.' Olivia at last managed to halt this tirade. 'Leon, listen to me. If I marry again, I forfeit all my rights to the corporation.'

'You're not serious!'

'I am!' Olivia's breath bubbled with excitement. 'Oh, darling, didn't Adam tell you? If I marry again, I get a settlement of three hundred thousand pounds, but that's all! After that, everything is held in trust for Henry's grandchildren—grandchild! Sacha!'

Leon could hardly take this in. 'Are you sure?'

'Of course I'm sure. But since the only man I knew I would ever want to marry was—as I thought—forbidden to me——'

'Oh, Liv!' Leon's defences crumbled, and with a groan of submission his mouth sought hers. 'Liv, Liv,' he muttered, pressing her so closely against him, she could feel every bone in his body, 'I didn't know how I was going to live without you.'

Some time later Olivia, snuggled drowsily into the curve of his arm, stirred sufficiently to say: 'I wonder why Adam didn't tell you about that clause?'

'Can't you guess?' Leon's hand moved possessively over her thigh, drawing her closer against him beneath the silk sheet. 'Knowing Adam as I've come to know him, I'd say he kept that back deliberately. I guess he was afraid I might be prepared to marry you, to achieve my own ends.'

'If he only knew!' Olivia gurgled with laughter.

'Hmm, well—he may not be all that pleased.'

'I think he'll be very pleased,' declared Olivia firmly. 'After all, he was fond of Alex. And Alex's son will eventually take his rightful place in the organisation.'

'Poor little devil!' remarked Leon dryly. 'I don't envy him. But Lilian's got a sensible head on her shoulders. She'll make out.'

Olivia moistened her lips. 'Francis will help her.'

'Yes.' Leon hesitated. 'I suppose he's another one who won't be too pleased with our arrangements.'

'Francis has been a real friend,' said Olivia, nodding. Then, abruptly, she levered herself up on one elbow to look down at him. 'Leon, could we propose Francis to act as Chairman—until Sacha is old enough to vote?'

Leon's brows arched. 'I don't see why not. You do have the casting vote, at least until we're married.'

'Yes.' Olivia smiled. 'I'm sure Sean Barrett would agree.'

'I'm sure he would.'

Olivia sighed. 'The corporation will be safe in Francis' hands.'

'Which isn't exactly what you wanted.'

'Nothing was exactly how I expected,' said Olivia wistfully. 'And it was all so long ago. It's become—clouded.'

Leon nodded. 'Well, it's obvious that both Alex's father and your mother had reasons for reproaching themselves. Whether they did or not isn't important now. What is important is Sacha—and you and me.' He grinned. 'Not necessarily in that order.'

Olivia looked down at him. 'At least they brought you and me together.'

'For which I can forgive them almost anything,' Leon agreed softly, his eyes caressing the rounded curve of her breast. 'Now, can we get some sleep? Or do you want me to look haggard in the morning?'

'What do you want?' asked Olivia, allowing herself to slide down against him, and Leon decided that he could stand a few more dark circles round his eyes.

Masquerade
Historical Romances

Intrigue excitement romance

THE KING'S FAVOURITE
by *Caroline Martin*

When Sir Gavin Hamilton is spurned by the lovely Honoria
Somervell he vows to bring about her downfall. To his surprise
he is unable to carry out his threats. Can it be that he needs love
more than all the things he has fought for – power, wealth and
the king's favour?

PIONEER GIRL
by *Margaret Pemberton*

To the small band of pioneers struggling towards the Rocky
Mountains in the bitter winter of 1846 the chance meeting with
Major Dart Richards is a fateful encounter. And to the
orphaned Polly Kirkham it is especially disturbing. But the
Major has vowed never again to become involved with a
woman, so why does he find himself accompanying them
across the icy wastes in pursuit of an ideal?

Look out for these titles in your local paperback shop from
9th April 1982

Mills & Boon
Best Seller Romances

The very best of Mills & Boon Romances
brought back for those of you who missed
them when they were first published.
In April
we bring back the following four
great romantic titles.

THE GARDEN OF DREAMS
by Sara Craven
Lissa wasn't quite sure whether or not she really wanted to marry
the attractive Frenchman Paul de Gue, so she was glad to accept his
invitation to visit the family château and meet his relatives.
Unfortunately this also involved meeting the austere Comte Raoul de
Gue – who made it clear that he did *not* want Lissa marrying into
the family!

VALLEY OF THE VAPOURS
by Janet Dailey
If Tisha didn't get away from her domineering father soon, he and she
were going to come to blows! So she went off to spend a long holiday
with her sympathetic Aunt Blanche – and met Roarke Madison, who
was even fonder of telling her what to do than her father had been!

THE REBEL BRIDE
by Anne Hampson
Judy hadn't in the least wanted to marry Chris Voulis, but in the
time-honoured Cypriot way the marriage had been arranged for her.
'Start as you mean to go on,' a more emancipated married friend had
advised her – and accordingly Judy had refused to be a real wife to
Chris until they knew each other better. She had won the first round
– but couldn't she still lose the game . . .?

THE BEACH OF SWEET RETURNS
by Margery Hilton
The little beach had been Kate's childhood paradise. But she returned
home to Malaya, a successful model, determined to make no
sentimental pilgrimages. For ever since her first unhappy love affair
Kate wore the cool assurance of her career as a defence she vowed no
man would ever break down. But she reckoned without
Brad Sheridan . . .

ROMANCE

Variety is the spice of romance

Each month, Mills & Boon publish new romances. New stories about people falling in love. A world of variety in romance – from the best writers in the romantic world. Choose from these titles in May.

NORTHERN MAGIC Janet Dailey
MASQUERADE WITH MUSIC Mary Burchell
BURNING OBSESSION Carole Mortimer
MORNING ROSE Amii Lorin
CHARADE Rebecca Stratton
BLACKMAIL Penny Jordan
VALLEY OF GENTIANS Margaret Rome
THE PRICE OF PARADISE Jane Arbor
WIPE AWAY THE TEARS Patricia Lake
THE NEW OWNER Kay Thorpe
TOO HOT TO HANDLE Sarah Holland
THE MAGIC OF HIS KISS Jessica Steele

On sale where you buy paperbacks. If you require further information or have any difficulty obtaining them, write to: Mills & Boon Reader Service, PO Box 236, Thornton Road, Croydon, Surrey CR9 3RU, England.

Mills & Boon

the rose of romance

ROMANCE

Variety is the spice of romance

Each month, Mills & Boon publish new romances. New stories about people falling in love. A world of variety in romance – from the best writers in the romantic world. Choose from these titles in April.

NOT TO BE TRUSTED Jessica Ayre
THE OVERLORD Susanna Firth
WAIT FOR THE STORM Jayne Bauling
DAREDEVIL Rosemary Carter
THE SEA MASTER Sally Wentworth
BITTER REVENGE Lilian Peake
TROPICAL KNIGHT Lynsey Stevens
LONG COLD WINTER Penny Jordan
SHADOWED STRANGER Carole Mortimer
SMOKESCREEN Anne Mather
LOVE IS ETERNAL Yvonne Whittal
THE ICICLE HEART Jessica Steele

On sale where you buy paperbacks. If you require further information or have any difficulty obtaining them, write to: Mills & Boon Reader Service, PO Box 236, Thornton Road, Croydon, Surrey CR9 3RU, England.

Mills & Boon

the rose of romance

Mills & Boon Reader Film Service

See your pictures before your pay

Our confidence in the quality of our colour prints is
such that we send the developed film to you
without asking for payment in advance. We bill
you for only the prints that you receive, which
means that if your prints don't come out, you won't
just be sent an annoying credit note as with the
'cash with order' film services.

Free Kodacolor Film

We replace each film sent for processing with a
fresh Kodacolor film to fit the customer's camera
without further charge. Kodak's suggested prices in
the shops are:

110/24 exp. £1.79
126/24 exp. £1.88
135/24 exp. £1.88
135/36 exp. £2.39

Top Quality Colour Prints

We have arranged for your films to be developed by
the largest and longest established firm of mail
order film processors in Britain. We are confident
that you will be delighted with the quality they
produce. Our commitment, and their technical
expertise ensures that we stay ahead.

How long does it take?

Your film will be in our laboratory for a maximum
of 48 hours. We won't deny that problems can
occasionally arise or that the odd film requires

Mills & Boon Reader Film Service

special attention resulting in a short delay.
Obviously the postal time must be added and we
cannot eliminate the possibility of an occasional
delay here but your film should take no longer than
7 days door-to-door.

What you get

Superprints giving 30% more picture area than the
old style standard enprint. Print sizes as follows:

Print Size	from 35mm	from 110	from 126
Superprints	$4'' \times 5\frac{3}{4}''$	$4'' \times 5\frac{1}{8}''$	$4'' \times 4''$

All sizes approximate.
All prints are borderless, have round corners and a
sheen surface.

Prices

No developing charge, you only pay for each
successful print:
Superprints   22p each.
This includes VAT at the current rate and applies to
100 ASA film only. Prices apply to UK only. There is
no minimum charge.
We handle colour negative film for prints only and
Superprints can only be made from 35mm, 126 and
110 film which is for C41 process.

If you have any queries 'phone 0734 597332 or
write to: Customer Service, Mills & Boon Reader
Film Service, P.O. Box 180, Reading RG1 3PF.

One of the best things in life is...FREE

We're sure you have enjoyed this Mills & Boon romance. So we'd like you to know about the other titles we offer. A world of variety in romance. From the best authors in the world of romance.

The Mills & Boon Reader Service Catalogue lists all the romances that are currently in stock. So if there are any titles that you cannot obtain or have missed in the past, you can get the romances you want DELIVERED DIRECT to your home.

The Reader Service Catalogue is free. Simply send the coupon – or drop us a line asking for the catalogue.

Post to: Mills & Boon Reader Service, P.O. Box 236, Thornton Road, Croydon, Surrey CR9 3RU, England.
*Please note: READERS IN SOUTH AFRICA please write to: Mills & Boon Reader Service of Southern Africa, Private Bag X3010, Randburg 2125, S. Africa.

Mills & Boon
the rose of romance